Five Words

Sally Measom

Five Words

First edition printed in the United Kingdom 2024.

A CIP catalogue record of this book is available from the British Library.

ISBN (Paperback): 978-1-7396167-1-7
Imprint: livelifeyourway
Typeset design: Matthew J Bird
Poem 'Warning' Copyright © Jenny Joseph, SELECTED POEMS, Bloodaxe 1992. Reproduced with permission of Johnson & Alcock Ltd.

For further information about this book, please contact the author:
www.livelifeyourway.co.uk
sally@onehappyplace.co.uk

For everyone who wishes they could have
one more conversation…

To Richard + Janice,

Remembering all
the great times
with your mum +
dad.

x

Main Characters

Sam - Youngest son

Dan - Sam's older brother

Mike - Sam's dad

Maggie - Sam's mum

Maisy - Sam's girlfriend

Shaun - Sam's best friend

Jody - Maisy's friend

Cassie - Mike's friend

Part I

"The Start of Everything"
2016 and 1995

Maggie

I don't know who I was,
I don't know who I am,
who is Maggie?

2016 - Sam

Hi, I am Sam and I'm going to tell you the story of my family and how life changed for me forever.

We came here from a large city over four years ago and it was a big change. A new job at an insurance branch for Dad, and a smaller school for Mum to teach at. It was a good opportunity for us all, moving back to where Dad grew up. We were looking for an alternative future and trying to make new friends, Dad was full of hope and handshakes, saying goodbye to the old neighbourhood and hello to the new. My brother Dan and I were outwardly smiling and sad inside, we convinced each other it was for the best because Mum and Dad were happy.

Dan and I have never been a problem, we are easy teenagers, we respect Mum and Dad and neither of us is the sort of teenager who wants to cause a scene, partly because of the effort involved in all the drama.

It wasn't that far in miles from where we were, but it felt like another country at first, moving from the place we used to call home, where we knew everyone, every shop in town and all the bus routes. It felt like we had moved to the other side of the world.

At the old house all my friends lived on the same street less than 20 doors away, this was like another planet.

My new school was different and exciting, and changing at 11 was not so difficult, a few people who didn't know anyone joined at the same time as me. It was worse for Dan trying to fit in two years above when friendships were already in place, but he settled in and made some friends in the end.

It has been a good move, we knew starting anywhere new would be hard, I am good at things, so it helped me to settle in quickly, playing in sports teams and finding the schoolwork easy.

I'm a good allrounder, not the most popular at school but a long way up the food chain. I chose my friends carefully and we are a tight group. Maisy is now my girlfriend as well as one of the group, she was the first person I spoke to on my first day at the school. I never expected us to get together back then, but I've known for at least a year she was more than a friend. It took her longer to work that out and ages for me to move out of the friend zone. We still hang out a lot, the four of us, me, Maisy, Shaun, and Jody.

So, a bit about Maisy. She is cute not in a sickly annoying sort of way, she's more likely to punch me on the arm than walk around holding hands, but I know she likes me, she tells me all the time. When Maisy smiles, she makes me want to smile, and when I make her laugh it's as if the sun comes right out of her and I feel alive in her sunshine, it's warm and familiar. It's a place I want to spend my time, she makes me forget everything else for a while and I need that more than ever.

I still can't believe this is my life. I was nearly 16 and my birthday party was finally happening with my three closest friends, Mum and Dad would be there, it should have been a great night, a night to remember. I'd decided to order in pizza and sit outside in our garden, Dad had put up fairy lights and birthday balloons were everywhere. We had pulled a couple of tables together and were laughing and joking, planning to watch the sun go down.

A week before my party, I was up early and found Dad alone crying in the garden. Dad never cries. He saw me and said we would catch up after the party and asked if Mum had been the same as always with me. The answer was yes and no, she was doing all the normal things, going to work, making dinner, cleaning the house, and maybe asking the same questions more than usual about school, homework, and my life.

I didn't think much about it, but I didn't think much further than my own orbit back then. Anyway, looking back Mum had been acting a bit strange, Dad said she was tired and needed regular lie-downs, she was asking us both random questions and talking loads about her parents. She was tense, wound up, distracted, quieter and a bit sadder maybe, but it could have been anything.

My party started at 7pm and before everyone arrived Dad was trying to calm Mum down; she was getting anxious because she didn't want people to come to our house. I could hear hushed voices through my bedroom wall as I was getting ready. Dad was explaining why they were coming as if she didn't know, it was odd, but I was too wrapped up in how I looked to process anything. Dad was dealing with it, and I knew it would be okay, Dad always sorts everything out.

Just after 7pm my friends arrived, it was a beautiful sunny summer evening perfect for being outside and talking about the rest of your life. A prosecco toast to me and a couple of ciders each, we were making plans for next year, it was not just my birthday it was nearly the end of exams, so we were all celebrating. All that work and years of study come down to a piece of paper with the right letters on it to get us the ticket to our future. I managed to put that thought out of my mind ready to enjoy the night.

The pizza arrived and I remember thinking it was all so good, feeling part of something, these friends, this place, my future, it felt so normal and I was happy living my dream not wanting to be anywhere else right then.

Mum came out into the garden from the kitchen and I'm talking to Maisy. Maisy looked edgy more grown up, definitely more grown up than me and I'm touching her arm and she's laughing at my attempt at a joke, I remember thinking this is where I fit, with Maisy, right here right now.

"You can't go out with her she's black!"

They are the words that shattered my life and changed my world as I knew it.

As I turned to look at Mum, behind her eyes there was somebody else or nobody at all I couldn't tell the difference back then.

Everything went into slow motion, there was silence, Dad was ushering Mum inside, and everyone was looking at me for an explanation.

Dad came outside red-faced with tears in his eyes, and my friends' faces changed from shock and disbelief to sadness and pity as their fear reflected back at me and we realised something was terribly wrong with my mum.

At 16 the world ticks by and you are front and centre stage, obviously it's your time, and the future is yours for the taking until suddenly it isn't about you anymore, it's about surviving, coping, making big decisions, being responsible, never feeling normal again because you don't fit anywhere. Your life and your problems are so different to everyone else you know, and looking after your mum and dad will become your only priority, how is that fair?

From that day, nothing has been the same, it's the day I understood Mum as I knew her was never coming back, Happy Birthday Sam.

The day after my party Dad came into my room. I knew he'd been up most of the night I could hear him moving about and I was awake as well. He sat on the end of my bed, head in his hands and then looked me straight in the eye and said, "I don't know what will happen next."

We sat for ages in our own heads neither of us knowing what to say or do. Then Dad said Mum wasn't going back to school, and I tried not to imagine how bad things must be for Mum to give up the teaching job she loves.

Mum slept for hours the night of the party and was back to being more mum-like again when she came downstairs the following lunchtime.

I'm sitting in the kitchen when Mum and Dad begin to tell me what they have known for a few years, Mum has Alzheimer's and is never going to get any better. They didn't want to tell me until after the party and my final exams had finished. Her disease had other ideas, no more hiding it's here to stay, and more outbursts are expected as she begins to operate more regularly without a filter.

Mum looks like Mum but she's quiet. I'm not sure she knows exactly what's going on, she looks like she's trying to physically shrink herself into the chair. Dad says there are seven stages of Alzheimer's, and they think Mum is at stage four, meaning technically speaking she is in moderate decline whatever that means.

I feel cheated, why didn't I notice and why didn't they tell me?

And now I find out Dan knew, he's more perceptive than me it seems, and he'd started asking questions, so they had to tell him.

Why am I reacting this way, they didn't lie to me, but they didn't tell me the truth either, I was left out. Apparently, they wanted things to be as normal as possible for as long as possible, what did they think I would do, am I so weak they have to hide things from me?

This must be what shock feels like, everything inside me has changed and started shifting around.

All the things I thought I knew, the pieces that made up my life don't fit together anymore. I want to hit something or someone and run and shout and kick and hide but I say nothing. I get up to leave, I need to be outside, the kitchen is oppressive, and I can't breathe or think with them in here.

My solution is to head around the corner to Shaun's house and hammer on his door until he gets out of bed.

Shaun is built like a bouncer, tall and broad, he towers over us all at school, only his face hasn't caught up yet. He comes downstairs in childish pyjamas, dishevelled, blinking, asking where the fire is.

When you enter Shaun's bedroom you enter another world, the curtains are always closed so the sun's not on the TV, and it's always dark. Everything is all over the floor, clothes, plates, books, trainers, it's an obstacle course and one I'm used to. Maybe he's so messy because he's so smart, and the order that goes on inside his head means it has to spill out somewhere or he would explode with all that neatly filed knowledge tightly packed into his brain. His life is still the same and I don't want to talk about my life now I'm here. We take up our usual positions on the floor in Shaun's bedroom playing Call of Duty on his Xbox, and for a few hours, I forget everything and concentrate on killing.

It's only when Shaun wants some food he asks if everything is alright. He knows I don't want to talk about it, I shrug, and we go back to the Xbox. Just being here feels good and I don't care if I'm avoiding being at home, I can't do anything to make it better so there's no point being there. I head home early evening having managed not to talk or think about things for most of the day.

This was day one when the news first landed in my brain, the disconnected numb feeling started on day one and lasted for months.

Maisy relentlessly texted me all day and I didn't reply to any of them, finally, she phoned at night, and I answered her questions, each with one syllable, I don't want to talk to her right now.

Time seemed to pause after that for a while and all I could think about was how was it okay for Dan; he was escaping, leaving me and Dad behind to cope with everything. I know I sound selfish and it's not his fault, but I would do anything not to be here. Dan gets to go to uni and start a shiny new life and the rest of us get a new life we don't want.

Dan's always looked out for me, we've never had the same friends or hung about in the same group, but I know he would step in if I needed him to. I took it for granted he would always be here to do that, I never thought it would ever change, I never thought about a lot of things.

I am existing, getting up, going to school when I need to, eating lunch and dinner, and then heading back to my room as soon as I get in. Dad is busy anyway taking Mum for tests and visits to the doctor, hushed conversations go on all around me and stop when I enter a room, I don't want any details what's the point? I'm avoiding conversations, getting up at the last minute, running out the door, places to go people to see, too busy to talk, it's all bollocks of course.

It's been three weeks since my party and the news about Mum still doesn't feel real. Every morning I wake up hearing the same noises, the radiator kicking in, Pharrell Williams singing "Happy" from my alarm (ironic I know), and the water running downstairs while the smell of toast drifts under my door as it has done for most of my life, until I remember, after those brief moments of ordinary, that Mum is not normal Mum, and the trains collide in my head once more.

1995 / 2016 - Mike

It's 1995 and I am a pupil at Brook Hill Secondary School in Oxford in the second year of my A levels studying Business, English Literature and Language. I like studying them all, I think business will be the most useful though unless maybe you want to be an English teacher.

My part of Oxford is the suburbs and the world moves quite slowly here. On weekdays it's all about school and sports, at weekends it's more sport and some parties, I know it's tame by big city standards. My cousins in London say they come back here for a rest but I like it, I'm comfortable with the familiar.

I've been going to this school since the first year and not much has changed in my life at school or with my friends, we are all growing up together, some of us more quickly than others. I like school, the routine of it and I don't mind studying, I work best with a plan and being organised is a big part of who I am.

So, let me tell you about the day that changed my life.

You hear about one moment, a chance meeting, a happy coincidence where somebody's world changes forever, and that somebody on that day was me.

Up until this point, I had always thought my life was very average, my parents were average, and compared to my friends' houses ours was average. I was an average height and weight, and my life looked the same as everyone else's until I went to school on Tuesday 4th July 1995 and there was Maggie.

She was radiant, and with the light behind her she looked like an angel, petite and perfect in a purple batwing dress. She was the new supply teacher for English. The most amazing physical pull, chemical reaction and electrical charge collided, it was channelling through me, between us, when she stared back at me.

In the movies or when Disney do it best, this is the moment when the music starts, the doves fly, and the hearts appear. In my new experience, I felt sick, swallowed hard and managed a hesitant hello. I stood completely still rooted to the spot just looking at her as the world kept turning round and round, everything inside me was spinning upside down, landing back in a place that I didn't recognise, I had fallen in love, it was love at first sight.

I was abruptly brought back down to earth when one of my mates punched my shoulder, having asked me the same question three times, my mind was on Maggie.

She quickly became all I could think about, the only person to occupy my thoughts, I had never been so distracted by anything or anyone in my life. The world seemed brighter and the colours clearer, a muted tint had been lifted, and the true beauty of everything that was a secret before had been revealed to me. Getting to know Maggie was the only thing that mattered, I know I sound like some sort of lunatic, but I knew she would change my life. Maggie on the other hand was a calm and professional teacher tasked with managing a class of eighteen sixth formers and she moved into motivational teacher mode as she ushered us all into class.

The first time we had a proper conversation was a few weeks after that meeting, and I will spare you all the details because I can't remember a lot of what we talked about, and my small talk back then seriously needed more work. I stayed behind after class to talk about the assignment, but really it was to get to know more about her.

The headlines are she hadn't been teaching for a while, she had taken some time out and only moved to Oxford recently. The most important news was she didn't wear a wedding ring because she was single. So naturally, I offered to show her the sights, as casually as I could as if it was no big deal.

I planned to impress her with the real Oxford, the best coffee shops, the pubs, and the limited nightlife on offer. Research on my part into all the above was ongoing, sketchy at best, I didn't go out much but Maggie didn't need to know that. I gathered information from everywhere I could in a crazy fashion, I was treating the task like I needed to pass an A level, and she was oblivious, grateful for a kind student to be helping her settle into a new area. I later discovered her intentions were genuinely innocent, unlike mine. She had looked at me and felt a connection but not acknowledged or recognised it as the connection that would change both of our lives forever.

We first met outside of school at "Friends" coffee shop, just off the high street, yes, that honestly was the name, made popular by the TV series we were all raving about back then. I arrived first and wondered what to order to impress her, was hot chocolate too childish even without the marshmallows and sprinkles and did it make me appear less of a man?

I waited and spun the conundrum around in my mind like it was the greatest problem on earth, and when she sat down and ordered an americano I said I'd have the same and I didn't even drink coffee.

She had a jacket on which made me want to stroke it, anything to touch her. It was made from black velvet and she told me "Black Velvet" was one of her favourite songs from her uni days, it was to become one of our songs. I couldn't get over how perfect she was with her mischievous green eyes, a forest to get lost in, and her long dark hair, which I imagined brushing my face as another X-rated scene passed by. Her playful words and sarcastic smile kept me hanging on her every word and I had to remind myself to look away, to stop staring, everything was captivating to me, and I couldn't help falling in love with her, I had no choice.

It took her longer and she wouldn't entertain even kissing me until I was 18, but I knew she was the one even though she was 25 and I was only 17.

After six months of just being friends, casual coffee shops and the occasional drunken pub night, we started dating and became Maggie and Mike a couple, and I couldn't have been happier.

In 1996 when you were dating you were a couple from the start, none of this "we are just talking" or "friends with benefits" business, you were either seeing someone or you were not, it all felt simpler back then.

It was sad that the age difference sat like an elephant in the room, between us and nearly everyone we knew. They were either falsely polite or embarrassed to say anything to our faces and raised eyebrows were the norm. We ignored everyone, cocooned in our private world which left no space for anyone else's opinion.

The only time we noticed the age difference in a big way was with some cultural stuff, music I had never heard of and news stories I knew nothing about. I guess it's similar to meeting someone from another country whose experience of growing up is different to yours or someone who's lived a rural life meeting someone who's always lived in the city.

All our experiences are unique, but who Maggie and I were as people, our values, and the desire to be together were stronger than anything else, nothing could have stopped us from being together.

I passed my A levels; Maggie was still a supply teacher and we needed to decide what to do next. I didn't want to go miles away to university and fortunately, I got the first job I applied for, an apprenticeship at an insurance company. I had no idea what I wanted to do, but soon realised the order and process elements of the job suited me well and I was happy to stay on permanently when they offered me a job.

My job has always been a means to an end, it pays the bills and allows me to have every weekend off to spend with the family. Some would say I am not driven and haven't pushed my career very hard, however, I am comfortable with what I do, and I don't need a big title or to kill myself for a salary to feel good about myself. How much time we chose to spend together was one of the best decisions we ever made, because of what is happening to us now.

The first time I brought Maggie home to mine was for Sunday lunch, and she said she was so nervous she couldn't eat. Mum tried her best to be normal and was anything but, she was using her telephone voice sporadically and preparing cauliflower cheese to go with lunch to show Maggie how sophisticated we were, we'd never had cauliflower cheese before. Dad nodded and grunted as usual, mainly from his position behind the paper and tried his best not to get involved.

Maggie was not what Mum had in mind for me her only child, she was too old and my teacher and Mum couldn't understand what we talked about and had in common. She wondered why I didn't want to play the field more before settling down ideally with a local girl my age.

They both tried for me though Mum and Maggie, and Mum never thought Maggie had done anything wrong unlike some of the people that were bending Mum's ear. I had talked to Mum about her almost from the start and I was 18 and had left school, only going back for my exams by the time we started dating. To me Maggie was everything I ever wanted, I never imagined I could feel that way and we were so right together.

Maggie and I talked about our life in the past, present, and future, about our previous relationships, and how surprised we were to fall in love with each other. Maggie had only had one other serious relationship, she was engaged for a few years, and they were together for about four, she had been on dates since, but nothing serious. I'd had three girlfriends from school, so I wasn't exactly a beginner in the relationship and sex department, they were all my age and in my year. I chased one of them for ages believing I was in love. Looking back I liked them all but that's as far as it went, and I was still speaking to them afterwards so no big dramas, they faded out mainly due to a lack of effort on my part.

Meeting Maggie and falling in love obviously meant taking off all my clothes at some point. I worried about this more than I should have done, and I was constantly replaying revealing my skinny, still developing boy/man body to her. It kept playing on a loop in my mind as I imagined standing there feeling the most vulnerable I had ever felt in my life, it would take a few beers that first time.

We had talked about being ready, and to be honest, I had been ready from day one, Maggie wanted to be sure, and the longer I had to think about it the more nervous I became. I overthink things and procrastinate for far too long and this gave me plenty of sleepless nights waking up from dreams I struggled to forget. I played out in my head several thousand times how it could all go wrong, torturing myself, I was desperate not to disappoint her.

In the end, Maggie could see it in me, as I would come to realise, she could see everything. It felt as if she could look through my eyes into my soul and ask the right question to drag me out of myself, away from doubt and indecision and into the confident and capable world she existed in.

When it happened it was sex, but sex with love attached and that made all the difference. The slow enjoyment of each other's bodies was exquisite, we practised frequently as you do when you are in a new relationship, and we learnt to relax and trust each other completely. The joy I felt when I took her to that other place, and the desire she awoke in me, made the greatest plays and novels written about the power of love finally make sense.

A few years later we got married, I was twenty and had never been more ready for anything, it was the biggest year of my life, we got married and our first son Dan was born.

The wedding was a small one, our choice, it was full of whispers a bit too loud, to let us know who thought it wouldn't last. We didn't care, it was about the two of us and I was so in love with Maggie I felt invincible, on top of the world, the only person who had ever felt this way. I knew what real love was and it was Maggie shaped, she was mine and I was hers and the rest of our lives stretched out before us, it was the opening of our play, Act 1, Scene 1 and we were ready to begin.

When Dan arrived life became much busier, we learnt how to be parents and adjusted to no sleep and becoming a three, then Sam was born two years later and our life was complete. Life was good, we loved each other and worshipped the boys. I was working hard and enjoying it and Maggie was happily teaching. Money was okay and although we were sometimes tired when they were younger, we both had evenings and weekends off and Maggie had all the school holidays to spend with the boys.

We went on holiday every year, usually to the seaside, down to St Ives or up to Whitby and we all enjoyed being together, it seems such a simple uncomplicated life when I think back.

When Maggie's mum died, she left her some money and we moved back to where I grew up. The boys changed schools and it was a good move for us all.

When we first saw what is now our house, we knew it would be our home forever. We were moving back to the area where our relationship had first started. My parents were not far away so we would be able to help them more as they got older and they could be there more now for the boys, it was ideal.

Time raced by as it does when you are busy and then when Maggie was 43, she started forgetting things.

Test after test revealed it wasn't an early menopause, stress, anxiety, overwork, or any other number of potential diagnoses, it took a year to find out she had early onset Alzheimer's. It was only because Maggie persisted with the local doctor that we found out at all. Finally getting the life-changing diagnosis was the ultimate hollow victory. I got fed up with hearing people say "It's uncommon in someone so young" as if that made it better for us somehow.

Maggie and I talked, cried, shouted, and discussed every way it wasn't fair when we first got the diagnosis. We were regularly up all night going over the same ground driving ourselves mad, falling into bed exhausted wanting our old lives back, hopelessly looking for them and finding them inhabited by new people. I couldn't understand why it had to happen to us, as if we'd done something wrong to upset the gods and brought this on ourselves somehow, I was looking for someone to blame.

No matter how much I ranted at the injustice the outcome was the same, we were devastated but needed to find a way to begin to live with it or we would destroy the precious time we had left together.

2016 - Maisy

I think my life was pretty ordinary until Anna was born. I couldn't wait to have a sister and waiting for her to arrive felt like forever. I had been an only child for nearly ten years, most of my friends had brothers and sisters and I couldn't wait to show her off. Mum and Dad knew it was another girl from the scan and me and Mum spent two weeks painting her room in girly pink and purple before she arrived, we only repainted it last year because Anna loves blue.

Dad is from Antigua and Mum is from Peckham. He is tall, confident, and loud and says exactly what he thinks, and Mum is small, cautious and quiet and contemplates things. You couldn't get two more opposite people than my parents. Although Mum doesn't say much what she does say is often cloaked in her own disappointment. You know where you are with Dad, with Mum I am never quite sure.

It's easier since Dad left, Mum seems okay, I guess it's one less person to think about. Anyway, Anna is now six and can't be carried around anymore. It's obvious to anyone she's different, the wheelchair gives it away. She is funny and clever, and she gets away with more than I do, it's just that her legs don't work. She doesn't think the same way as me, in a lot of ways she might always be about six in her head. It's not easy when you expect one thing and get another, no one knows what to say to me about Anna. If they say they are sorry I hate it I don't want them to be sorry for me or for Anna, I wish they wouldn't say anything. I'm not sorry she's my sister, we do loads of things together. I don't mind looking after her, I'm helping out more now it's the three of us and I try to look after Mum too.

I need to keep us all happy and I need to pass my exams, I'm constantly juggling between home, school, Sam and my friends. Dad says he worries about me but I don't see him much so he can't be that worried.

I don't get a chance to go out very often and Sam's party was keeping me going, a night off from my life, a chance to spend some time with Sam and the others before my final exam.

I loved going to his house, everything was always tidy, not immaculately tidy, homely tidy, with a comfortably lived-in feel. His parents were like the families you see on TV adverts all smiley and perfect with proper smiles that reach their eyes. His mum and dad still had lots of kissing going on, it was embarrassing at first when Sam's mum hugged and kissed Sam and then me. I got used to it quickly though and it felt safe, a big hug that lasted and a kiss on both cheeks every time I used to visit like she'd not seen me in years. She kissed his dad in front of us too, Sam always looked embarrassed, but I didn't care.

I've been seeing Sam properly after the "just talking" phase for nearly a year, we are an item, boyfriend and girlfriend. He can be quiet, and he thinks a lot, it's hard to get him to talk to me sometimes and I wonder what spins around in his head. When he does let me into his world I try to remember to listen, and not to speak all the time because what he does say is usually smart and worth the wait. He makes me feel special, he trusts me, and I trust him. I can be my giddy, awkward, goofy self around him, and he doesn't mind.

For Sam's 16th party, I'd had my nails done in bright orange with gold stars at the top of each one because that's how I felt, like the star on the top of our Christmas tree. My dress was orange, my ridiculously high sandals were orange and gold making me nearly six feet tall.

I don't want to show off, but I did look good for me, who spends most of my life in joggers, hoodies, and big trainers. It reminded me of when I was little digging through the dressing-up box trying other people on for size, and imagining what it would be like to be them and do their job. Putting on the princess dress and strutting up and down in their life made me feel important, more confident, silly really, it's only clothes. Even my hair went right, and it's got a mind of its own, so you never know.

Mum took a photo I think she was surprised at how I looked, Dad always calls me his "sunshine girl" so the orange fits with how he sees me, and I felt glowing inside and out that night when I set off for Sam's house.

When I arrived, I could tell he was impressed. He said he was proud that I was his girlfriend and publicly announced that I looked gorgeous, then whispered that I looked fit, which gave me a million butterflies.

I sat down next to Jody with a glass of bubbles in my hand, relaxing and breathing in the powerful perfume from the flowers in their colourful garden.

We chatted about exams, our plans for the summer, and what we wanted to do next year. I still hadn't decided and didn't want to think about it that night. It was perfect sunny weather and being with my best friends like that I couldn't imagine us not being together forever.

Sam was busy opening his cards and presents, he loved the gold chain that I bought him and put it on, it looked great with his black Nike T-shirt.

We all clapped when the food arrived, and one minute we were eating pizza slightly tipsy and the next his mum said something terrible about me in front of everyone.

I love his mum and dad and couldn't understand what was happening, everything moved in front of me turning into a place I couldn't recognise. I left straightaway, his dad was crying, and I didn't see his mum again, I didn't understand what was going on. I took my shoes off and ran out of there embarrassed and confused, Sam didn't follow but Jody was shouting after me and I kept running.

Mum looked shocked at my mascara-streaked face when I burst into the house hours early with one foot bleeding. She stroked my hair as I cried into the sofa cushion for hours and tried to explain what I didn't understand.

I messaged Sam all the next day, he didn't even bother to reply, I was so worried.

When I got to speak to him at night, he didn't want to talk to me and couldn't wait to get me off the phone. He managed one short sentence and said his mum has got Alzheimer's some sort of memory disease. When I asked Mum what it meant she chewed her lip as she explained that his mum was never going to get better.

How is that possible when his mum is so young and looks so healthy, it's terrible, but it's not my fault. I've spent the week trying to understand more about what it means so I can talk to him and try to help him. When we catch up later it will be the first time I've seen him on my own since the party. Mum says just listen to what he has to say, but I'm not sure how I can listen if he isn't saying anything.

I thought it would be easier if we went out for a walk, and as I get nearer to him, he looks as if he hasn't slept for the whole week. I have never felt as awkward with him as I do right now, we have always been relaxed around each other, and that's what I loved about us it was so easy. I don't know how to be around this new version of him, subdued and emitting sadness from every one of his pores. I know he is tired but am I expecting too much from him to acknowledge I am here?

After an hour together he leaves to walk home and doesn't look back. I am relieved to see him go. I'm scared for us. Does he want to end it and he can't tell me? I know the stuff with his mum is awful but how does it help if he pushes me away?

Mum says to be patient and I don't have a choice if I want to be with him, but I can't go to his house now it's so frustrating, I will have to wait for him to come to me and I'm not good at being patient.

I hardly ever come to Jody's house even though she is my best friend, apart from Sam, usually.

Jody is the image of her dad with jet-black hair, bright blue eyes and pale skin which looks translucent and violet when she's cold. I've only seen her dad a couple of times in all the time I've known her, if she's at mine and it's late, her mum always comes to pick her up.

Jody and I live very different lives in very different houses, she lives in a big house where everything matches. It's on a fashionable private estate with neat trees and matching front gardens the type of perfect house you see on American TV shows.

When I go over there, I feel untidy, I don't fit into her world, and when she comes to ours Anna makes it hard, so we spend time at school and at weekends when we can, meeting outside at the park or down the rec. I don't have much free time left with Mum, Anna, and Sam to share it between and Jody swims for the school which takes up loads of her time. Her mum is always kind to me though when I visit, and she always looks perfect, a model mum with immaculate hair and painted nails.

As soon as I take my shoes off she tries to feed me, and she usually sends me home with baking for Mum and Anna when she has made extra which is most of the time. Everything in their house is decorated in shades of grey and their fancy kitchen is huge, their table seats twelve, you could almost get our whole flat in here I think, as we help ourselves to some home-made chocolate cake.

Jody is an only child and says she gets lonely sometimes, she doesn't have to do her own washing or clean her room, they have someone who comes in and does lots of jobs. It is always so calm at her house and my house is always loud and chaotic, but I wouldn't want the silence that surrounds all the big empty spaces here.

We sit on the floor in her bedroom with Tom Daley covering the walls, looking as if he might dive into her room and join us at any moment, and I worry about getting chocolate buttercream on the pale grey carpet. I talk about Sam, and we come up with endless reasons why he is behaving this way and why he can't or won't talk to me. I hate talking about us in this way it feels disloyal to Sam, we have always been good together and I thought we could be honest with each other and talk about anything.

I leave Jody's house with cling film-wrapped chocolate cake, not feeling any better than when I arrived, still not knowing what to say to him or what to do next.

2016 - Mike

If you didn't know Maggie well, you would think she was completely normal today, she looks like the picture of health, her face is saying one thing, cleverly betraying her brain and what lies beneath the surface.

As I look around, she is the youngest patient in the waiting room by at least twenty years, I silently acknowledge this as I sip my orange-coloured machine tea.

We move into a private room and sit close to each other in the claustrophobic chemical-smelling space, while the well-meaning consultant tries to get my head out of the sand and explain in some detail the prognosis of Maggie's disease.

Just five words, random ones she had to remember and repeat, that's all it took two years ago to test Maggie's memory and realise something wasn't right.

I am looking at the floor, hoping to melt into the busy pattern on the carpet so I don't have to listen to what I know will be news I don't want to hear.

Maggie has insisted we have this appointment, she wants me to hear straight from the consultant what it will be like living with her so I can prepare for our future, for what's inevitably going to happen, to get me to understand how her illness will affect me and the boys.

When he leaves the room, I know the old Maggie is unhappy with me when she says "I bet there are not many appointments where they go in to talk about a patient's future and end up talking about the European Union! You've got to start accepting things, Mike."

I don't want to hear it yet, I needed to create a distraction, after his first sentence "It's not good news and it's not going to be easy."

He went on to say Maggie as I know her, will no longer be Maggie, she will be completely different and need full-time care as the illness progresses, and it is progressing quickly, so I swiftly changed the subject, I didn't need to hear anymore.

The injustice of no one to blame for the diabolical cards that fate has dealt us, with no clear path through this, or concrete conclusion in sight, leaves me at a loss.

How am I supposed to know what to do or say? I always fix things.

The rage and helplessness I feel because something is taking her away from me and I can't stop it, was not for that room. It's tightly bound inside me for later, calmly waiting to unravel on its focused path of destruction, like a bomb sitting quietly waiting for the timer to bring it to life.

After the disastrous appointment, Maggie took control when we were sitting on the sofa one night, and started the conversation we had been dancing around for weeks, her words rehearsed and coming out in a rush.

We both knew the conversation we needed to have but were unwilling to admit it was our future, as if our acknowledgement would make everything happen faster.

Decisions must be made, but once we had committed our thoughts out loud there would be no going back.

How do you say and do the right thing?

We tried.

Different versions of words that had been going around in my head rise to the surface and we are brave and honest when we speak.

"What will happen when you don't know who we are when you don't recognise us anymore?" I ask.

Maggie has always been the brave one, and I know she has thought about this for a long time, when she produces two brochures for nursing homes within a thirty-minute drive from home. She is making me promise not to be her carer, she wants me and the boys to have a life of our own.

She has investigated what will happen to her and how things are likely to progress, as the best journalist would research the facts of a story. She has spoken to people, doctors and other health professionals and has an A4 checklist of pros and cons for each nursing home, it's the same meticulous process she uses when we are choosing where to go on holiday.

She is very clear, and caring for her full-time is not what she wants for any of us.

I object and selfishly cry. I have been crying regularly recently, another thing that is out of my control. I can't imagine her not being here with us with me looking after her, that was what we agreed when we got married, for better or worse, in sickness and in health, I am not prepared to let her down.

She is crying now and keeps saying being her carer is not what she wants for us, and she should be allowed to make this last big decision for herself while she can.

I can't process it, sitting there with tears streaming down my face, I can't contemplate a life without Maggie here in it every day. I can hardly remember the time before her, before us, my life was smaller then, she is the love of my life, she has taught me so much and we have grown up together in many ways. I was the younger one in years, but she was young too from her limited experiences in life. Now I am heading for a life that is out of control, full of despair and impossible decisions, not knowing what is right and what is wrong anymore.

She has been the best wife, is the best wife, why has my mind started to think in the past?

It's my safety net I think because I cannot imagine a future for any of us. The pictures that Maggie and I painted, the places we would visit after the boys had left, joking about our ever-expanding bucket lists, picturing us in our sixties travelling through Europe, having our gap year.

Dan and Sam maybe getting married one day and the type of partners they might choose, the grandchildren we may have and where we would take them, discussing the sort of parents our sons would become and the two of us growing old disgracefully.

Maggie always insisted she would dye her hair purple and wear lots of inappropriate clashing clothes to shock everyone from their prejudices and preconceived ideas. She would never conform just because of her age, like the lines from her favourite poem which has been on the wall in our kitchen for years. I will never know how disgraceful we would have become; I suspect she would have been more outrageous than me with all her choices.

Warning

by Jenny Joseph

When I am an old woman I shall wear purple
With a red hat which doesn't go, and doesn't suit me.
And I shall spend my pension on brandy and summer gloves
And satin sandals, and say we've no money for butter.
I shall sit down on the pavement when I'm tired
And gobble up samples in shops and press alarm bells
And run my stick along the public railings
And make up for the sobriety of my youth.
I shall go out in my slippers in the rain
And pick the flowers in other people's gardens
And learn to spit.

You can wear terrible shirts and grow more fat
And eat three pounds of sausages at a go
Or only bread and pickle for a week
And hoard pens and pencils and beermats and things in boxes.

But now we must have clothes that keep us dry
And pay our rent and not swear in the street
And set a good example for the children.
We must have friends to dinner and read the papers.

But maybe I ought to practise a little now?
So people who know me are not too shocked and surprised
When suddenly I am old, and start to wear purple.

There is no time like the present Maggie says, she is trying to be jolly, and make light of the situation as we get into the car, and I lock us in. She used to do this false jolly voice with the children if they were heading for the dentist or the doctor, maybe I am the child at this moment.

We are heading for our first visit to two nursing homes, it's the exclusive club you don't want to join and a place no one wants to become a part of their lives.

Fear and trepidation at what we might find set up camp in my brain as we silently head towards the unknown.

2016 - Maisy

Sam walks past me in the upstairs corridor at school and I've had enough of the silent treatment, what is happening with his mum is not my fault and I shout at him and tell him how unfair he is being, while a line of moving spectators listen in the background.

"You've had 16 years with your brilliant mum and dad, it's not enough, and it's never going to be enough, but you can't change what is happening now. How does shutting me out help anything? Bad things happen to other people too. There is no perfect family, if you ever bothered to dig beneath the surface you'd see we all have problems and manage to carry on without making everyone else feel bad. We get it wrong and make mistakes and sometimes what happens is nobody's fault, there is no one to blame no matter how hard you look, but we keep on living and dealing with it. You've made this all about you, it's fine to be sad, it is unbelievably sad, but other people are hurting too. This is the worst thing that has ever happened to you, remember it is happening to all of you so stop playing the only victim. I'm done with trying to talk to you to help.

Have you ever stopped to think about what my life has been like or how I feel?

What's happening to your mum is terrible, hideous, awful but do you think my life with Anna is easy and that I don't think about when my parents won't be around to look after her? Should I be her carer for the rest of my life or have a life of my own and if I do choose a life away from Anna is that selfish, she's my sister where will she live, I love her, but should I always put her before me?

Grow up Sam, look outside yourself, and get out of your own head, yes, it's sad, it's awful but you are hurting everyone who loves you."

I run past him with my head down, furious, as some of the spectators begin to applaud. I find Jody in the toilets.

Between loud sobs I cry the tears that have been building up for months, I'm still ranting when she hugs me to calm me down. Sam is so frustrating, why do boys never talk about anything?

2016 - Shaun

Becoming Sam's best friend came as a surprise because we were not too keen on each other at first. I thought he was a bit of an idiot and a show-off, now I know he's just confident, easy-going and knows who he is, he was the most sorted of all my mates.

He has parents who love each other and want to be together, unlike mine, not that I'm complaining Dad left a long time ago. I don't hate Dad. I hate the way he treated Mum, but I know he regretted hurting me, eventually, when his conscience kicked in long after his sex drive had slowed down.

As a group we are all good friends, it's more awkward since Sam and Maisy got together, Sam and I still hang out though just the two of us. It's more difficult because Jody likes me, she's always liked me, but so far only I know that would never work out.

Sam knows party nights are not my thing and I'm not good at lots of questions and meaningful conversations, confrontation makes me anxious. I am happier in a small group or with my head in a book or role-playing on the computer where pretending to be someone else is easy. I always choose the loudest and most opinionated characters and create a glamorous backstory, the complete opposite of my life.

Since I was 12, I've known that I'm gay. I thought about it before then, but this was when I knew for sure. At junior school I didn't understand myself or realise the way my friends were starting to feel about girls was different to the way I felt, it's not as if you can see inside your mate's head to check you all think the same. But I knew when they started talking at secondary school about who they fancied and what they wanted to do to them it didn't feel the same for me.

I spent months trying to like any girl the way they did, I kind of already knew it was never going to happen. It's my news, and I will tell everyone soon, Sam first and then Mum when I'm ready. I'm not ready yet, I want to wait and get through my exams first, it's not an excuse, I don't need the distraction or the barrage of questions and the not-so-hidden disappointment that will inevitably follow from Dad.

I'm sure of one thing, it's my life and I will live it my way, on my terms, with whoever I want. Dad has shown me that, wife number three before he was 40, at least this one's better than the last, closer to his age and she doesn't want to make friends and talk to me all the time to impress him.

If I keep working hard my expected grades should see me sail through to Oxford or Cambridge in a few years. It's great to be smart and it comes reasonably easily thanks to Mum's genes. She had a great job as head of research in a laboratory, it paid well and she loved it, but the hours were too long, and she couldn't do it part-time, so she had to leave when Dad left.

I don't think she's ever switched off from that job in her head, and she will never forgive Dad for having to leave it, the job was easily a bigger loss than he was.

When Sam's party arrived, I was looking forward to it, I enjoy being at his house it's one of the few places I relax, and I was ready for some downtime with a few drinks to switch my brain off from all the studying and who doesn't like free pizza?

I had a few drinks at home first, smoked some weed on the walk around and was happily relaxed by the time I got there, I was the last to arrive.

I tried to get out of there as soon as possible when it all kicked off, they didn't need spectators and I'm not one of those people who has to look back for casualties when they drive past a road crash. Sam knows where I am.

Walking Jody home that night seemed the right thing to do. She chattered on endlessly about what might or might not be happening at Sam's house and I successfully tuned her out most of the time.

2016 - Jody

Finally, he's noticed me the way I wanted him to.

I can't believe at last he sees me the way I've seen him since I was 12, he's the only one I've been interested in. I have imagined how it would feel to be with him and how perfect we would be together for the last five years of my life.

I'm well aware that I'm the least clever in our little group, it doesn't bother me. They want to study for more years than I do and have big careers, I don't know what I want to do yet but I know it's not that.

You can meet someone at my age and still be together all through the uni years, so even if Shaun goes to Oxford or Cambridge and I stay here it can still work out. That's what happened with my mum and dad, they met at school, so there's no reason Shaun and I can't be those people. Stay together, settle down in our twenties, and have two children ideally a boy and a girl, and they won't be lonely, they will always have each other to talk to.

We can happily spend the rest of our lives together now he knows I am the one. I knew it would happen eventually, I just had to wait and be available, be there for when he was ready.

Over the last few years he's worked so hard to get top grades he never made time for anyone else romantically speaking. I didn't expect it to be tonight though, straight after what happened at Sam's party, I guess I was all dressed up and looking older, maybe that's why he looked at me differently and saw me as more than just Jody, and you can't hide what you feel.

That's why life can be so fantastic, one minute every day is ordinary, each one the same as the last, and then unexpectedly something magical happens.

For our first time, I hadn't expected to do it in the woods behind my house, in all the scenarios I thought about, this wasn't one of them.

Shaun was walking me home. He offered to walk me back which was a kind thing to do, and I felt relaxed walking through the woods with him. I don't walk home the woods way at night, but being with him always makes me feel safe.

He stopped to kiss me, and I knew he'd had a few drinks and smoked something because I could taste it on his breath, I'd had a few drinks too but still, when we kissed, I knew that finally we were both ready and

I couldn't stop smiling inside and out. This was it, the start of us.

It was awkward finding the right spot, somewhere quiet where no one would see us, but I know the woods well. I've lived in the same house all my life, built dens in the woods, played hide and seek in them and all those childish games I loved, but now they are the place where Shaun and I made love.

It was the first time for me and I was nervous, but I didn't say anything. I talk too much, and I know I can be annoying so I thought it would be good to be quiet.

It wasn't what I expected, it was uncomfortable wet and messy, maybe it gets better with practice, but it was worth it because when Shaun lost control right at the end I looked into his eyes, and knew he loved me the way I love him.

Afterwards, I lay on my back on the damp grass and looked up through the trees at a patch of fading light. The trees were grand columns from some ancient time with branches crisscrossing high up in the sky. I felt part of something bigger than me, surreal and otherworldly, secure, safely surrounded by this ancient woodland, protected by it, with Shaun by my side I was ready to take on the world.

Nothing is as I expected it to be, Shaun is ignoring me and I don't know why.

I've only seen him briefly at school since Sam's birthday night, I guess he is busy revising for his final

GCSEs, most of the school is acting like their life depends on passing them.

I know boys don't hang around with their girlfriends usually at school, but he's not spoken to me at all, I'm surprised and disappointed after what happened between us.

I hate exams, they make me anxious, it's not the grades that worry me the most, it's sitting in that room trying to understand the questions and remember anything I'm supposed to write down. I know it at home but looking at everyone else who knows what they are doing makes my mind go blank and I convince myself I can't do it. I fail every time in the "Who's got the best memory test." I can't cope with the pressure, sometimes I am physically sick and shaking before I go in.

It is getting to me, I'm not eating, and I'm worried I will fail everything, and I've missed my period but they're usually all over the place, it will sort itself out, I will be fine after the exams. Maisy called round after our French exam today, the exams are nearly over thank goodness, only Psychology left next week for me.

She tells me about the horrible thing Sam's mum has got and how she won't know who he is soon, and I feel like crying for them all. I can't imagine what we would do if it was happening to my mum, I couldn't live without her.

Maisy and I haven't caught up as much as usual because she's had stuff going on at home and she is trying to support Sam, although she says he's in a terrible place right now. I've told her about my night with Shaun, keeping it to myself for a bit felt right, secret, and made it more special, not that Maisy would gossip, she's not like that but I'm never sure what she tells Sam. Anyway, she knows now and didn't say much, I thought she would be pleased for me, but when I mentioned my period, she looked shocked and said I should do a pregnancy test.

It's Saturday morning, although technically it's nearly lunchtime, and I am getting breakfast when Maisy arrives, she's brought a packet of pregnancy tests with her.

We read the instructions and I wee on the plastic stick. A few minutes later we know that I am pregnant, how is that even possible?

I've only had sex once, we do another two tests to make sure and they all say the same thing.

All I can think about is that Shaun will have to speak to me now. I've been crying for a full hour and Maisy keeps saying the same thing over and over again, that it will be okay, and we can sort it out. It should feel reassuring, soothing even, but what does that even mean?

It's not that I had any great life plan in mind but being pregnant at 16 was never something I thought about. It's not ideal, but teenagers get pregnant and they survive, sometimes they say it was the making of them.

It's not like I'm smart or want to stay on at school or go to uni, it might be the best thing to happen to us, me and Shaun, young parents doesn't mean bad parents, does it?

I can't tell my mum and dad they will be so disappointed in me. I can't not tell them either because I'm not going to get rid of him or her.

Maisy's not saying anything as I verbalise everything as it comes into my head, the only thing she does say is I need to talk to Shaun because she's not sure he will see things the same way as me. Sometimes she's so negative and her relationship with Sam is not great at the moment, so she's hardly the expert.

I need her to be supportive and tell me she will be there for me and the baby. She's my best friend and I need her too. Sam is not the only one whose life is going to change, I know it's not the same but don't babies bring hope and joy, they are cute and fun.

Maisy thinks I should tell Mum and Dad now. I need to tell Shaun first though, that's the right order and maybe we can tell my parents together, me and Shaun then we can tell Shaun's mum. They will be cross, and I don't think my mum will want to be called Grandma, but deep down I know they love me and will help me sort everything out. Mum knows that I've liked Shaun forever.

Maisy hugs me again as she goes to leave and it feels awkward, nothing has changed between us but everything has changed for me as I am growing a new life inside me.

I look up from the bed and even my cat Poppy looks as if she is judging me, flicking her tail in an irritated fashion from her position high up on the windowsill.

She jumps down onto the bed, and it does comfort me to stroke her as she plods and paws for more while the reality of what I have done begins to sink in. We've had her since she was a kitten, she is long-haired and a tortoiseshell colour, my beautiful cat, you can see where she's been in the house, she leaves cat hair everywhere.

I would have loved a brother or a sister, at least I have Poppy and I can talk to her. I think I might work with animals when I leave school, maybe I can find a nursery for the baby.

The last thing I do at nearly midnight is message Shaun, I say we must meet tomorrow, it is urgent, and I don't want to talk about it over the phone. He agrees to meet but says he hasn't got long, he's revising.

So, we met, and I told Shaun.

I rehearsed what I was going to say all the way there, but in the end, "I am pregnant" is what came out first.

He was quiet and didn't show any emotion but he never does. He sat and listened and didn't say I shouldn't have the baby, he didn't say anything much, so I think that's good.

I filled all the gaps in the conversation, I can't help but fill the spaces between other people's words, anything is better than the awkward silence. Of course, it's a shock for both of us and we will get through it together, at least he knows now.

Maisy called round to see how it went, I started to feel very sick, so she didn't stay long. I am relieved he knows, now we can plan things and work out how and when to tell our parents.

2016 - *Shaun*

I am waiting on a bench near the ice cream van when Jody arrives, and as I watch her purposefully striding towards me, I get a sinking feeling.

I have been successfully avoiding her after that night, it didn't mean anything to me, but I'm not sure she sees it that way and more importantly, she is distracting me from precious revision time.

God, I'm selfish, Jody is telling me she's pregnant and it's mine, and all I can think about is going to university. This won't stop me, I'll still go, my life has been mapped out that way forever, and I am not changing it.

As she cries and looks at me for some support, I can't give her the reaction she craves, I don't have it in me, so I say nothing. I have no words to respond to her and I can't tell her how I feel. It's the only time I've slept with a girl and I don't know why I did it, Sam's party was such a weird night. I didn't plan it, it just sort of happened, one minute we were messing about in the woods and the next we'd hooked up.

She is always so desperate, maybe I thought it would make her night, or maybe I didn't think at all. The sex wasn't memorable, it was quick and served a purpose, not something I want to do again with a girl, and now Jody is sitting here telling me she's pregnant, but it will all be okay because she has worked it out.

She has planned how the three of us can play happy families and is telling me that a baby doesn't have to change things, lots of teenagers do it, I tune out after this part for a while. I honestly think she's convinced herself we will be the next Brangelina, she doesn't know me at all.

I look upwards, it is uncomfortable continuing to look at her, and I imagine jumping on a passing cloud and floating along in the blue sky to another country, somewhere hot, being anywhere except here.

She goes on and on about our perfect little life, the idea has taken root in her head, it's sprouting rapidly and growing fast as she describes the new life she has created for us without consulting me, it's absurd, being this desperate is never attractive.

I can feel my face trying to say something as I am dumbfounded by her stupidity, this is not a life I will be living. I am struggling to control the feelings that are starting to bubble up. I'm frantically tapping my leg, something I do when I am frustrated and need to release the energy in some way when I can't find the right words to speak. My jaw aches from the effort of clenching my teeth so I don't shout at her and tell her she is insane.

She hasn't noticed any of this and keeps talking more rapidly, and I wonder how she could be so stupid to get pregnant in the first place unless she wanted this to happen. And how could I be so irresponsible?

I realise how naïve she is, why didn't I notice this before, she is so young and needy, she seems a few years younger than the rest of us. I'm still not speaking, and it is taking a monumental effort not to shout, not to show her the repulsion that's going on inside me as I try to keep my passive mask on.

The incredulity I feel in this situation makes me want to explode in her face, the fact she is so deluded and living in LA LA Land, on another planet, in another universe, it's sad. I wish I was anywhere but here, and I have to get away from her before I say something I will regret, I need to think on my own. Sitting on a bench near the local shops is not the place to cause a big scene, I hate everyone looking at me and people keep glancing at us as they go in and out of the shops in their ordinary lives.

Jody is not speaking quietly, and her gestures are big, interspersed with some tears, people are making up their minds about what is going on. I think about everyone else's life unchanged waiting for them at home exactly as they left it before they came out this morning. Mine is not mine anymore it is somebody else's, it belongs to a stupid, careless idiot.

I've spent my whole life in control of things, planning my life, using my brain and it's a great brain, making sure I am nothing like Dad. Now I have landed myself in a scene from a crap TV soap, the one Mum is always watching, and I take the piss out of, this is the sort of mess that belongs to other people's lives.

Finally, she has stopped talking, and I get up to leave, telling her I need some time to think, and I am left with a bunch of feelings I don't want to own.

She nods in such an understanding way it makes me want to hit her to wake her up from her fantasy fairy story.

I run and keep running, back to the woods, not near where it happened, right across the other side where it is darker and more crowded with trees tightly packed together and overgrown brambles.

I stop in the darkest part and lean my back against the biggest tree then slide down its trunk until I am sitting down. Head in my hands and furious with myself I cry, and I can't say the tears are for Jody or the baby, they are big selfish tears for me and my life.

Reality hits me a few hours later when I get home and walk through the front door. I walked out earlier thinking my last two exams were my biggest problem and now I am going to be a dad, it's ridiculous this is not my life.

I don't want a baby and I don't want Jody. I can't think about it, I need to focus on my exams, get the grades and plan what to do next. So, I do what I always do and put it in another compartment marked "later" in the corner of my brain and carry on as before.

2016 - *Sam*

I am going to see Maisy after we argued at school, well she shouted, and I didn't say anything.

She is furious with me and I have to sort it out, I've never seen her so cross. She's never shouted at me before; I can't believe I've never thought about what it's like for her at home. She's always so happy when she's with me, I feel anxious.

I am racing to the bus stop and getting on the bus taking the stairs two at a time, I sit down, shit, tears are streaming down my face.

A well-spoken lady is asking if I'm alright, she is speaking to me kindly and she's about the same age as my mum. I am thinking STOP TALKING, I want to shout it at her because she is making me cry even more.

What is wrong with me, why can't I stop crying, people are staring. I am embarrassing myself; everyone is looking at me, I need to get off this bus. I push past her to get off at the next stop, it's about three stops from town.

I am running towards the park to a bench near where Mum and I used to feed the ducks when we first moved here, it feels childish now, but we loved watching them waddle along with their ducklings.

I always liked coming here, I used to skateboard with my friends. I can't believe what's happening to my life.

It starts raining hard, powerful horizontal rain with a dark thunderous sky above me matching my mood, signalling the start of a big storm, it looks exactly how I feel. I sit down soaked and completely alone, everyone else has run for cover.

I've been coming here for over a quarter of my life, and I want to go back and do it again, remember it better and appreciate it this time, appreciate Mum. I want to go back to when Mum was fine, back before all this fucking crap started, I am so angry all the time.

It takes me another week to make it to Maisy's house. It is a bright sunny day the sort of day I would convince Shaun to be out all day, I'd call around early and drag him away from the safety of his bedroom. We would go to the park, meet friends, and maybe go fishing just the two of us. That life seems a long time ago almost as if it belonged to someone else.

Before I have a chance to ring the bell, Maisy's mum opens the door ready to go out with Anna. She invites me in and I awkwardly half smile at them both while trying to keep my head down, I don't want any questions as I move upstairs.

Maisy's room is full of posters with questionable quotes on, "Live, Laugh, Love" seems particularly appropriate today, I do love her.

Two of her walls are painted yellow, one is pink and the other is orange, it's a lively space, and I couldn't sleep in it every night. It's like a big bag of Skittles have thrown up over the walls, I have mentioned this to Maisy, but she loves all the bright colours. There's a dressing table under her window, full of perfume and make-up with beads and earrings hanging up everywhere.

Apart from the chaos on the dressing table the rest of her room is tidy, and she always makes her bed. Maisy's room always smells of sweet apples and nail polish, I think about Shaun's room and decide not to think about what that smells like.

She's got pinboards up with photos of her family and photos of us, she's the only person I know who still prints off photos. I enjoy looking back at our lives, my life, and my face up there before everything, the memories we've made are always on show. As I study them, I can see I look visibly different in the photos, my appearance has slipped along with everything else and I'm not sure exactly how.

I walk around looking for somewhere to sit, knowing she's still cross and I am stalling for time. She looks as if she's been crying, she is not going to make this easy for me and doesn't speak as I wander about.

I plump for the chair next to the bed, the bed feels too intimate somehow, too presumptuous.

"You look amazing!" I say, and she does, her dress matches her bedroom all pink, yellow and orange flowers.

"I'm a dick!" is my next line.

"Yes, you are!" is hers.

Ice broken, I apologise properly and promise to let her in more, to tell her how I'm feeling and to stop shutting her out, unlikely, but I need to get through this part.

She's nearly crying and I'm not sure if she's sad, happy or just relieved. She is beautiful and brilliant and hugs me tightly so I relax, I hadn't realised how tense I was.

I let her keep holding me, melting into her and breathing her in, my breathing slows down, she is making me feel calmer. The choppy short breaths from earlier when I was running out of air have gone, I can feel my shoulders drop and we stop to look at each other, really look and we both smile.

Then Maisy kisses me and I know what to do, I am comfortable in this place, it is familiar. I am kissing her back and I mean it, I'm saying thank you for still wanting me even though I'm a mess right now, I want you too.

We undress slowly at first, but I'm desperate for her so I can switch my brain off and escape. We're on top of her single bed frantically tugging and pulling off our clothes, smiling and laughing as we roll about. When I'm inside her instinct takes over. I know how to do this, we know how to do this, this is what we do, and I've never meant "I love you" more than I do right now.

2016 - Jody

When I woke up in the middle of the night I knew something was wrong. I felt between my legs, it was wet and when I smelt my hand I knew it was blood even before I put the light on.

There is a lot of blood. I run to the loo grabbing clean knickers on the way and more blood quickly fills the toilet bowl. I sit there cold and shaking as the water turns bright red.

I count the blue flowers on the white wall tiles from the line above the top of the bath, and I count the flowers down the sides. Then I times the number of tiles across and down together without realising I am doing it as my brain distracts itself, desperate to find something else to focus on.

I am not stupid, I know what this means, I am having a miscarriage.

I don't know how long I sit there gently rocking, mind blank, before I use a Tampax and place a sanitary pad on my clean knickers. The bleeding is still heavy as I go back to my room to sort my bed out. I take off my bloody nightshirt and the stained bedsheet, put clean ones on and get back into bed.

I am not going to be a mum after all, I want to talk to Shaun to tell him he's not going to be a dad to hear his reaction. I could message Maisy, but she won't pick it up until morning and it's only 2am.

I start to shake violently as the shock sets in, I didn't mean to get pregnant, it wasn't planned but I had got used to the idea and I imagined our new life, Shaun and me with our baby. I wanted that new life, and I wanted our baby to love and care for, and for Shaun to know how right we are together.

I lie awake for the rest of the night wanting to talk to someone and feeling empty inside.

I message Shaun first thing and he doesn't reply until 11am. I arrange to meet him in the park at lunchtime and we sit on the swings as I explain I am no longer pregnant. He is hard to read but I can tell he is relieved; he didn't want our baby.

I lean back and look up at the pale blue sky and I hear Shaun say he made a big mistake sleeping with me, it's as if he is talking to someone else. I don't have any words left for him and I need to be at home. I am tired out, but strangely calm, he will not see me cry again.

As I walk back home reality lands like a big stone in my already aching stomach. I know that Shaun doesn't want to be with me and get married, he has a whole other life planned, what was I thinking? We are not running off anywhere and posting our perfect baby on Instagram, we won't be living my storybook ending.

I almost make it home without falling to pieces, until I struggle to hold my hand still enough to unlock the front door and the tears begin to escape.

As the door opens, I fall inside and collide with Mum, I push past her, race up the stairs to my room and throw myself on my bed. Mum follows me in and takes my hand, she has beautiful hands they always make me feel safe.

Mum is holding my hand as she did when I was a little girl, stroking it to reassure me, squeezing it like when I learnt to cross the road and turning it over as she thinks. All I can do is look down at our hands, her beautiful rings, I can't speak yet and tell her what a mess I've made of everything.

Mum is talking, I can't focus on what she's saying but her voice is calm and reassuring and I will tell her everything. I've been stupid and naïve, and I know Mum will blame herself somehow, she will try to hide her real feelings from me so she doesn't make me feel any worse. The thought of how much she loves me makes me ache, as failure and expectation fight inside me to reinforce how badly I have let her down.

After I've told Mum everything, forcing the words out through broken breathing and non-stop sobbing, she tucks me in as she used to every night, and I revert to being her little girl again.

I watch the light fade through my window and I'm exhausted. I feel like I've been holding my breath for weeks without knowing it. I can see the hurt and concern in Mum's eyes and worst of all the disappointment.

It's not how I thought it would be telling her, she's not cross about what I did, she's sad that I couldn't tell her. That's worse, I've made her sad and she's quiet now, thinking and reflecting, it always makes me feel scared when my mum is this quiet.

In my defence, I hadn't known for long and I had to tell Shaun first, didn't I? I lost the baby anyway so what was the point in upsetting everyone?

I think I would have been okay after the miscarriage, and in a few more weeks life would have been back to normal. But today it was too hard to keep dealing with it on my own and I couldn't pretend I was alright, or lie to Mum, she knows me better than that.

We stay there marooned on my bed as it goes dark with our thoughts quietly revolving around us, and with nothing left to say I fall asleep in her arms.

In the morning Mum brings my breakfast in on a tray in case I am too ill to get up and make it myself, it's boiled eggs and soldiers and I feel about five again, she doesn't mention last night.

Then she says in her matter-of-fact voice, that we are moving over 200 miles away up north in less than four weeks. Dad has been offered a new job and his company will pay for us to rent a house until we sell ours and find a new one. Mum says we will try it, she says she wasn't sure before, but it will be good to have a fresh start and we all need a change apparently. I am not sure I do, it's clear that after what I've done I am not in a position to argue.

I can tell she is as scared as me, she doesn't welcome change, but her smiley mask is bravely on telling me it will be fine and I will make new friends and get a chance to start again. She is desperately hoping I won't make a scene and I can see she needs me to help her through this, and I will.

Obviously, I'm worried about leaving everyone behind, and I try to imagine not being here, living my life somewhere else. The more I think about it the more a popping excited feeling is starting to build up in my chest, like the popping candy you put on your tongue when it explodes. It's scary but at least I am doing something and going somewhere, and I get to reinvent myself and tell people only what I want them to know. I will be a brand new me.

Over the next few weeks, we start to declutter as we plan the move and Mum and I look at houses online. Dad still hasn't looked me in the face since Mum told him about Shaun. We are functioning as a family, just.

Mum's being over bright and cheerful with us both, jollying us along, and we are trying for her. All limping around injured, leaving a polite space between each other as we adjust to what I've done.

They look at me differently now without ever actually looking at me.

2016 - Sam

When I next see Maisy and Shaun, not at the same time but in the same morning, they drop the bombshell about Jody.

I watch Maisy twirling and tugging her unruly hair as she turns words over in her mind, trying to find the best way to say whatever she wants to say.

I know her well enough now to wait for her to speak. "Jody was pregnant, and it was Shaun's," are close to the last words I expect to come out of her mouth, it's just another thing I didn't know.

After I've finished questioning Maisy about the how and the when, Shaun arrives. I can't believe he didn't tell me before. He said in his defence, he thought I'd got enough to deal with, and it was all over in a couple of days. I wish he had told me though, it's worse knowing everything last. I don't feel protected from things, just left out and it's one more thing that makes me stand out, before Mum he would have been straight round to tell me about the things that were going on in his life.

When Maisy told me her version of events it was weighted in Jody's direction, full of emotion with lots about Shaun doing the wrong thing, and how Jody thought it meant something, Maisy is clearly worried about her.

Shaun's version of the same story is purely factual he could easily be talking about something that happened to somebody else, so I get two versions of the same story. He has distanced himself from it already, and moved on, which I imagine won't be so easy for Jody to do.

Everyone's life keeps changing so quickly, I guess we are all adjusting at a different pace to our changes and holding tightly on to our version of events for our life support.

Then it's on to bombshell number two, Shaun announces he is gay. I guessed this a few years ago and we have a brief and superficial chat about it. I don't care who he sleeps with why would I, it's probably the least interesting thing about him.

If I'm honest, it feels good to think and talk about someone else instead of Mum. The main parts in the drama this time are being played by Jody and Shaun and the supporting cast are the rest of us. We will adjust to the news, accept it, and carry on as before because our roles are minor.

Too many well-meaning people say they understand and know how you feel but they don't, how can they if they've never been in your situation and played the main parts?

Unless it's their big news and affects them personally, they have the freedom to walk away they don't have to live with it on repeat day after day. I will never say I understand what someone is going through to anyone ever again.

One of Maisy's posters on her wall talks about walking a mile in someone else's shoes, I presume to understand their life better and feel their pain. I think not for the first time, if anyone wants to swap shoes with me, I'd be up for it right now.

2016 - Jody

It's moving day and Maisy is here helping to put the last bits into the car, the removal van left hours ago. In the last few weeks, we have had loads of conversations to reassure each other we will always be friends, and we each have half of a silver friendship heart around our necks to stay connected.

I am crying partly because the actual day is here, I don't want to go, but also because we can't find Poppy. Dad knows better than to suggest we leave without her; he is pacing up and down the drive looking at his watch. Even Mum is flapping which is unusual and makes me panic even more.

A row is about to erupt which is the usual stress row we have every time we go on holiday, all rushing about to leave home and get to the airport on time. We always spend the first part of any holiday car journey in angry silence until Mum relents and speaks first, Dad and I can sulk for hours.

Maisy and I head to the woods to continue the search and she calls Sam to come and help. Sam arrives with Shaun, it's the first time I've seen him since I told him I lost our baby. He looks awkward but manages a half smile and I smile sadly back.

As Maisy and Sam wander ahead, Shaun asks me to sit down with him, he wants to talk. We sit on an old fallen tree trunk not far from where it happened that night, I don't think Shaun remembers where we made out, but I do.

We are sitting over a person's width apart, perhaps he thinks if he touches me, I might think it means something. When he speaks, I know he is sorry, he looks younger as he tries to explain. He is uncomfortable shifting his weight around and fidgeting, he can't sit still. I watch him rocking and rapidly drumming his fingers on his legs.

Basically, he doesn't know why it happened that night, he likes me but not in that way, it could never be in that way. Shaun tells me something he has only told Sam until now; he tells me he knows he is gay.

I can't rearrange my face in time to make him feel better, and why should I? My shock and disbelief are obvious. He is full of remorse about what we did and has questioned himself continually about why he had sex with me that night.

He never thought about how I would feel or what it might mean to me. He is trying to apologise, tripping over his words in his clumsy way, and I don't know if I feel better or worse when he finishes speaking.

When Maisy and Sam return, they look at us both expectantly, still sitting there, and I manage a resigned smile. Shaun looks as if he wants to be anywhere except here, with me. We get up in silence and continue to look for Poppy and I don't speak to Shaun again for a few years after this encounter.

Eventually, we are ready to leave for our new house over three hours later than planned, with Poppy secure in her basket on the back seat next to me. Mum found her locked in the garage unperturbed by her ordeal and our frantic searching.

I turn to look back at our old house and an edited version of my childhood comes crashing into my mind as something starts to loosen and shift inside me. I have wasted my time dreaming about my perfect life and waiting for Shaun for so many years, I will never make that mistake again.

Maybe I am running away, maybe we all are, maybe it will help us to deal with everything and maybe I can become someone new, lots of maybes for me to consider.

As we turn out of our estate towards the motorway, I imagine I am the main character in a book, and the page has turned, so I can reinvent myself in any way I want before the new chapter begins.

I spend the rest of the journey working out who I want to be, so I am ready to live my new life as soon as we arrive, I am not wasting any more time.

2016 - *Shaun*

Mum doesn't know anything about the Jody thing, and I want to keep it that way.

Jody's left and it's all over there is no baby, she doesn't need to know, and I will never be that irresponsible again. I nearly ruined my whole life.

Part 2

"Surviving" 2016, 1989, the 1990s, and 2017

2016 - Mike

In the end, picking the right nursing home was an easy choice, like when you are choosing which house to buy, it feels right. I don't think it's a rational thing, it's an emotional pull towards something, and you instinctively know if it's the one for you. You never know for certain until you move in and start living your new life, making the best decision at the time is all you can do.

When one person leaves a relationship it's a choice, it's usually sad whatever the circumstances, for one person at least, if not both. When your wife has Alzheimer's there is no choice involved, she disappears before your eyes, and gradually you recognise less and less of the person in front of you.

I should have told Sam earlier, but I was trying to protect him. He's only a child and keeping his world as normal as possible for as long as possible seemed the right thing to do. I'm not so sure that I was right, the shock for Sam has been massive, and on top of that, he was dealing with exam pressure and feeling excluded when we knew about her illness.

Is there ever a right thing to do, a good way to break this sort of news to your family, knowing your children will be left with a mother they don't recognise and who doesn't recognise them?

Maggie still looks like my wife, and I don't feel differently in the way I love her. I feel more protective, she's always been so vital, present, encouraging and loving, but piece by piece I can see my Maggie seeping away with all the bits that make her Maggie leaking out of her and going to God knows where.

I have a million questions, the sort of questions you don't ever want to ask, like when you are first learning about sex and you're not sure if it's the way it's supposed to be, and what is normal, and are you doing it right the same way everyone else does it?

When I think about sex now with Maggie, one question keeps turning over in my mind. Is it wrong to sleep with my wife even though she doesn't know who I am sometimes? The question will not go away, it's shooting around in my brain looking for an answer, the right answer.

Emotionally I need to know she's still there, still my Maggie and that she needs and wants me the way I want her. But rationally is it wrong, when she knows who I am less than half the time in an average day?

Am I taking advantage of her, she is vulnerable, and I should be protecting her, but should I be protecting her from me or is it still acceptable to be intimate? My mind will not stop spinning, it's an annoying record on repeat, playing the same track again and again until someone presses stop, only I can't find the right button to press.

We've always had a great sex life, clung onto each other when things were hard, cried together, fell out, made up and had fun exploring and enjoying all of each other. I'm still human and I haven't changed but Maggie has, so is it wrong?

I move on to a practical task to distract myself from my current thoughts, I need to be doing something to occupy myself. "Try to connect people with what is familiar" a leaflet I skimmed through at the doctor's advised, it said that connecting with the past can be helpful to trigger a memory.

We've got boxes in the loft that haven't been opened for years, we moved them from the last house to this one unopened and there are some from before we were together. Wading through the past is not my idea of fun, reluctantly I climb the ladder into the loft that we always thought we would convert into our bedroom, and I pick up a box and pull back the tape.

I've opened a box with some of my childhood toys in it, Action Man has survived along with some Air Fix and Meccano that I built years ago, the models are cruder and more basic than you get nowadays. Combined with my toys are some of the boy's favourites that Maggie must have saved. I'm not sure Teletubbies, Power Rangers and Ninja Turtles would ever get on in the real world. It reminds me of watching Toy Story with the boys each toy special to someone once. I'm not sentimental about this sort of stuff, I loved it at the time but was always ready to move on, I didn't see the point of always looking back when there was an exciting future to explore.

When Maggie first told me she was pregnant before we got married, I don't think my reaction was the one she was expecting, it wasn't the one she wanted. I know I looked shocked, I tried to be excited, but she knew me so well she could see I was apprehensive, and it was obvious I didn't know if it was a great idea.

We were planning to get married anyway and I was hoping we were going to have some time just the two of us before any children came along, they were firmly planted in the distance for me. I knew Maggie wanted a family, but we weren't trying, it was a careless surprise, I know people say that, but for us it was true.

It took me a while to get my head around the idea, so when we went to the first scan at about 12 weeks and there was no heartbeat, I was shocked at how sad I felt. Two weeks earlier we had been standing in Mothercare looking at cots and prams, I had entered into a world I knew nothing about and thought I would know nothing about for a few more years.

However, I had got on board and accepted the inevitable and I was working out what kind of father I was going to be. I am not particularly close to my dad, he didn't do anything wrong, but he left Mum to do everything, a lot of dads did back then. She played taxi, driving me to Scouts and sports clubs, so it's not surprising I grew closer to her, and it's stayed that way.

She's spent all her life feeding me and cheering from the sidelines. When I thought we were having a baby I imagined myself in his role, I was going to be cool and definitely not the strict one, that would be Maggie. I was sure I could be better than my dad and more involved with my child's life, a friend as well as a parent.

I was unbelievably naïve and that was a good thing, if I'd known the reality of actually being a parent and the enormity of being responsible for another human being, I might have said no. I presume we all think we will be better than our parents if we feel short-changed in some way.

As we sat in the hospital desperately hoping something was going to flicker with life on the screen the nurse's face told us everything, we had lost the baby. I was more upset than I thought possible, grieving for someone I would never get to meet and never have the chance to get to know. I guess that's when I realised it was something I wanted as much as Maggie, to have a child that was ours so we could shower it with love, and we had plenty of love to give.

When Maggie was pregnant again, neither of us dared talk about it for the first three months. We didn't imagine and plan everything like we did the first time, we got through the longest few months of our lives together until we saw the heartbeat at the first scan.

The relief was palpable, it didn't mean we were out of the woods, we knew things could happen further on, but for the first time in a long time, we had some hope. And hey presto our son was born, if only it was that easy, he was late and had to be persuaded to appear and Maggie was ill for a while afterwards, but we coped.

Our son Dan was the most amazing thing I had ever seen, I couldn't believe we had created something so perfect and a whole new type of love miraculously appeared in my heart.

Going through the next box full of records brings back memories, Queens Bohemian Rhapsody is at the front. It was played at the end of our wedding ceremony as we walked back down the aisle and out of the church, it was extremely controversial at the time. Maggie did a great job persuading the vicar it was a good idea. We had a track from the Beautiful South as our first dance, it was one of the first bands I took her to see before we were officially an item.

Hunting under another two boxes at the very bottom of the pile is a box marked Maggie. I take a deep breath and open the perishing yellow Sellotape.

It feels like an intrusion, this box is from before we were together not that I think Maggie has anything to hide, but she should be here saying it's okay, giving me permission to open it. I decide I'm her husband, so of course it's okay.

The top layer is full of small dolls the type you collect on holiday from different countries, all in national costumes. Spanish flamenco dresses that were once bright red, with fragile lace that might disintegrate if I touch it.

Underneath the dolls is a large margarine tub with costume jewellery in it, it's the sort of jewellery a teenager might have worn in the '80s, big colourful plastic beads and massive gold-coloured hoop earrings, Madonna-esque.

At the bottom are some books including a Jackie annual, some Enid Blyton books and a box set of The Lion the Witch and the Wardrobe, as well as what appear to be Maggie's diaries. They are diaries, the first one is from 1981 it's blue with a penguin on the front with hardly anything written inside it.

There is some clear large well-spaced neat children's writing with an entry on 1st January 1981 reading -

> I am going to write in this every day. I want to be in a choir and on television like St Winifred's school choir on Top of the Pops. I got this diary for Christmas.

As I flick through more pages I learn about after-school gymnastics, various fallings out and making up with friends I have never heard of, and shopping trips with mixed results on Saturdays with her mum.

A final entry in August says -

> I am going on holiday to Cornwall tomorrow, I am soooooo excited and need to go and pack now!!!

The next diary is from eight years later, Maggie would have been about 18. I stop and read an entry from a much younger version of Maggie, one that I only recognise snippets of.

10th January 1989

I am not sure why Tom has picked me, the captain of the uni football team has asked me out. He's tall dark and handsome, fit, cute and looks at me with suggestive eyes. I need to be more confident and think of clever things to say.

Why can't I be one of those people who can think on their feet with quick replies and smart comebacks? So many of the other girls are cooler than me, they have more style, are more worldly, and have more experience with boys. I have a few more days to panic about what to wear and to work out if I should wear my hair up or down.

The girls in my group are nearly as excited as me about the date, one of them already goes out with one of Tom's friends. I need to write a list of everything I need to do before Friday and put the hairdressers at the top.

13th January 1989

I am excited, too excited and have to keep repeating to myself "I can do this" to get the courage to go on this first date, but I'm ready, so it's now or never, Pizza Hut here I come!

I'm back and it was brilliant!

As I closed my bedroom door and ran downstairs on the way out, Especially for You was playing on the kitchen radio and it suited my mood perfectly, Mum shouted, "Enjoy it" and Dad said nothing. I hummed the tune all the way into town feeling giddy, I don't need to share my secret love of Kylie and Jason with the world though.

I spent all the way there checking my reflection in every shop window and practising my casual smile, I nearly bumped straight into Tom outside the restaurant I was so distracted. We went in together and he held the door open for me which was kind, I think he knew I was nervous. I felt sick and had to sit on my hands so I couldn't bite my nails, I didn't think I would be able to eat.

Tom looked great, casual and sporty in a polo shirt and chinos, he knows his style and puts a lot of effort into what he wears. He was quieter on his own, we both had a deep-pan pepperoni pizza and a Coke, I ate about half of mine and Tom finished it off. I didn't know what to say at first, so we talked about all the people we knew at uni and then moved on to TV and sport, we had quite a few things in common. When he looked directly at me, he did this sideways smile and then he tipped his head to one side, and I felt like we were the only two people in the room it was weird, and I got butterflies in my stomach.

The time went really fast and he laughed a lot, I don't think I am very funny, he said he thinks I am cute. Tom paid for us both and asked me to meet up with him again next *week. I like him and I think he likes me; he said I was beautiful as he walked away, I can't remember anyone ever telling me that I am beautiful.*

As I scan read more about their developing relationship, I think that this is what a jealous partner does on a phone now, collecting evidence, trying to discover something they don't like and shouldn't be reading. This has nothing to do with me, it was a long time before we met but I can't stop reading it.

I pick up the diary for 1991 it has a serious brown leather cover and is embossed with gold lettering across the front.

Inside it reads…

He is at mine nearly all the time now, the rest of the flat are complaining he should pay towards the rent. I can't wait until next year when we finish uni and we can rent somewhere, just the two of us like a proper couple. It will be so good to spend time alone, we never seem to get any us time.

Tom often stays up later than me drinking with the others, I don't mind, I can't cope with the hangovers and need to get a good degree, so I have the best chance of getting a teaching job.

As I skip through the diaries from the early '90s there's nearly half a decade held in very few pages, the years have varying amounts of entries. Maggie seems to have recorded key moments, sometimes going for months without writing anything.

I look for something positive and more cheerful, if she wrote it down maybe it's lodged deep within her brain somewhere and reminding her of it will help to bring part of her back to us.

22nd June 1992

It is exciting to be renting our own place finally, we've had lots of trips to Ikea which I like more than Tom, I have to bribe him with the meatballs.

We've bought a starter pack of crockery and a selection of pans although I don't know which one to use for what, and we have a new black leather sofa. The flat is small but it's ours and it's starting to feel like home.

Tom still can't find the sort of job he wants so he's taken a bar job for now. I've got my first teaching job starting in September which is great, the school is not far from uni or the flat, so I know the area well, it's perfect. Everything is coming together I feel like a proper grown-up!

5th September 1992

I didn't realise a class full of teenagers could be such hard work, it's challenging and I'm a bit out of my depth. I need to be on top form to cope with them. They know I'm new, but I don't think they know this is my first proper job since I've qualified. When the head introduced me to the rest of the school in assembly, I turned red, I tried to confidently smile and look the part, but I still felt like a pupil. I can't believe I am in control of classes on my own, I ask them to do something, and they do it, most of the time.

The other staff have made me welcome, a couple are close to my age and helpfully steered me away from sitting in someone else's chair in the staff room and from using their mug. I am enjoying it and think I will settle in here, dealing with the parents will be the scariest part of the job from what the other teachers say.

9th December 1992

We are getting ready for Christmas at school, and you can feel the excitement. The behaviour in my year group is getting worse and everyone is winding down and switching off before the holidays, nobody wants to work. The other teachers say it's always like this. I don't know what's got into them I've sent two pupils to the headmaster this week.

Tom's hours are a nightmare, he goes to work at 4pm and comes in at 1am and I'm getting up at 6.30am and teaching all day, so we aren't seeing much of each other. He's working at the weekends as it's the busiest time in the bar, and I'm trying not to complain that I don't see him, but it's not ideal. He says it's not worth looking for a proper job until January as no one will take him on this time of year and he's probably right.

31st December 1992 - New Year's Eve

Tom has proposed, we went to his bar and met up with a group of our old uni friends and it was like we were all still at uni on a student night out. I drank more than I have for ages, and we got some free drinks because he works there, he jumped on top of the bar, got down on one knee and proposed. Technically he was a lot higher up than I was so I had to look up at him but who cares, he proposed! Of course, I said yes, wow, I am officially engaged. I don't have a ring yet as he didn't plan to do it, he said it felt right at the time, and everyone clapped and cheered it is the best New Year ever.

9th April 1993

Tom is still working at the bar and out after work again with friends. I heard our door open at 4am, I hope he didn't wake the neighbours as well. At least he didn't bring friends back this time, it has become too regular to be woken up by strange voices in our lounge in the early hours.

When I get up in the morning I am frequently greeted by the remnants of cheese on toast spattered on the grill, crisps scattered everywhere and a selection of dirty glasses that haven't made it to the sink.

14th June 1993

I can't wait for the summer holidays to have some proper time off; we have hardly seen each other over the past few months. It will be great if I can get him to commit to a holiday. He is spending so much time at the bar and hasn't applied for another job in ages.

I still don't have an engagement ring, he says he doesn't have a weekend free to go and look for one when I suggest a shopping trip. I am trying not to be moody and to mind too much, he says I am hard work sometimes and I don't want to upset him.

10th July 1993

We are off to Greece for a week in August just the two of us. We both need the break, I can't wait to sit in the sun, swim, read and drink cocktails. I am going shopping for some sexy holiday clothes and two new bikinis to show Tom what he has been missing working at the bar all the time and neglecting me!

27th August 1993

Greece was fantastic, Tom likes to party more than I do, and he made friends with everyone at all the local bars. He even served behind the hotel bar one night, showing off, making the cocktails he makes back home. Everyone loved Tom he is a showman and loves to entertain, I am lucky to be with him.

I am sure people wonder what he's doing with me, he says I am being silly when I bring it up, but I can see the attention he gets and the surprised looks over at me when they know I am his girlfriend. I feel plain with all the confident showgirl types that flirt with him, Tom doesn't understand, and I know I should be grateful that he picked me. He does drink a lot but doesn't everyone on holiday, and I did have fun, I've got the best tan ever.

6th September 1993

First day back at school, how did the summer go so fast? It was impossible to get back into it today after so many weeks off and the children felt the same.

10th September 1993

I have survived the first week back and I'm getting quicker at preparing lesson plans and sticking to the timings thank goodness. I am not letting the pupils distract me and we are getting through the work we need to complete in each lesson.

I am more confident that I can do this job, and I am becoming a more capable teacher than I was last term. My confidence is growing, and it's exciting to be back and feel like part of the school, I'm not the new person anymore.

Tom however is quite distant; he was only too keen to get back to work at the bar.

As I keep reading more diary entries I get a sinking feeling, I know they split up otherwise she wouldn't have met me, but this relationship for Maggie's part at least, was more serious than I was led to believe.

31st December 1993 - New Year's Eve

This time last year Tom proposed, I still don't have a ring and we haven't started planning the wedding yet. I'm in bed with flu, Tom is working at the bar, not much of a New Year for either of us. Mum offered to come over and look after me, they never do anything at New Year, but I don't feel like talking to anyone.

1st January 1994

It's lunchtime and Tom still hasn't come home. I don't feel any better and when he eventually walked in at 4pm I started to cry. He looked irritated and said he went on to another party after work and fell asleep on their sofa, it's clear this is not up for discussion.

He has gone straight to bed after shouting "Why shouldn't I enjoy myself, there was no reason for us both to sit at home being miserable just because you are ill."

3rd January 1994

"We need to talk." Why are those words never a good sign?

I thought this was it, that I had found the one, and Tom would be my husband and the father of my children, but he has met someone else.

I shouldn't be surprised he's always out and comes home late loads, and he's hardly spoken to me properly for months.

I have been busy trying to be the best teacher I could be, giving everything to my job. Then coming home to cook dinner, so Tom had something to heat up when he came in late. I did all the food shopping, cleaned the flat at weekends and made sure the bills were paid on time. I was finding it difficult, and I've had no one to talk to, I've taken on every domestic role as well as working. Tom just worked, well obviously it wasn't just work as he's met someone else at work and wants to move out.

I don't know how I feel, apart from feeling numb. I am not the sort of person who likes big dramas or creating a scene, five years of my life gone, wasted on Tom and my future has been wiped out. We were the perfect couple at uni, perfect until real life happened to me. Tom is still living the student life and I can see how he thinks I have become boring and predictable, but one of us needed to be responsible. It's not fair and I can't think what I should do next. I can afford the flat on my own and he can't, so I guess I will stay here and carry on.

Tom wanted to go now, today, to move on quickly, "It's better this way" apparently. Better for who? I was shouting, which I never do, and I could see from his irritated face it was the last thing he expected.

We argued about who owned what, both claiming the things we bought together. I could see he'd thought about it in advance, he had walked through the flat already in his mind and planned what he wanted to take.

In the end, I didn't care, as he carried his sad little cardboard box around filling it with the remnants of our life together.

When the door closed it was like a physical jolt to my body, an electric shock culminating in crying rivers of tears over the whole weekend. I should call someone, but I don't know who to call, it was just the two of us for so long.

I don't want anyone else to see me this out of control. I need to be on my own and think about what to do next. I replay every memory of us when we were happy with its relevant soundtrack, and torture myself with all the things I did wrong.

5th January 1994

I managed to start the new term and am getting through each day by focusing on my job. I can cope until I come home and know that I have all evening to get through on my own.

I am embarrassed at how stupid I was, running around after Tom and neglecting any friends I had. Weekends are the worst, I don't know what to do with myself, it's not like he was here that much but I am not seeing anyone except at school now.

23rd January 1994

I can't believe what I did tonight, I am disgusted with myself. Not even three weeks since Tom left, I got out of bed where I had been all day, to answer the door. It was early evening and Diet Paul, Tom's friend was standing there with a bottle of white wine in one hand and a bottle of Diet Coke in the other. That's why we call him Diet Paul because he only drinks Diet Coke.

He said he had come to see how I was doing. I didn't want him to come in, but it seemed rude to shut the door when he had made the effort, so in he came.

I got the glasses as he sat on the sofa, made himself at home, and chattered about an outside world I couldn't relate to, having successfully distanced myself from everyone in the past few weeks.

Two hours later we were having sex on the sofa, he said he had always liked me, and that and the wine was enough to persuade me it was a good idea.

I'd only slept with Tom before, and I've no idea why I did it. I don't like him, and I can't even remember his surname, at least it was quick.

I remember looking up at the ceiling from my position on the sofa feeling completely detached from what was happening, while his body got more and more excited. How desperate am I for someone, anyone? Afterwards, it was awkward when he climbed off me and he couldn't get his pants on fast enough. He wouldn't look down at me, still laying there on the sofa, fully clothed on my top half with my pyjama bottoms around one foot.

He half-jogged to the door to let himself out whilst telling me it was probably best if we didn't mention this to Tom.

I am unravelling, I don't recognise the person I am becoming. I climbed back into bed to write this after showering and scrubbing my skin vigorously, it's red raw in places. I needed to remove all traces of what I'd done. His smell was the last to leave. I need to talk to someone.

11th March 1994

I am determined to stick it out at the flat, but I am struggling to work out who I am now I am not part of a couple. I was the boring one and realise that I lived in Tom's shadow for a long time. I don't know what I think about things, and I need to develop some opinions of my own.

I have joined the gym at the leisure centre, and a local weekend walking group to force myself to meet people and hopefully make new friends, it is nerve-wracking meeting new people on my own and I have forgotten how to make small talk.

I present a carefully edited version of myself to the outside world. At least it will force me to do something other than come back to this flat alone every night, rationally I know it is time to move on.

Lots of entries follow throughout March and April talking about going to the gym and for country pub lunches with the walking group.

Then in May a couple of Tom's friends joined the same walking group and Maggie has drawn a sad face next to the words she has written, and the entries stop again until the first week in June.

2nd June 1994

I am still not getting over Tom; I don't want to go out. A couple of the teachers at school said they are worried about me, telling me to go to the doctor, I have lost lots of weight and I feel sad all the time. I am still teaching okay though, that's the only thing keeping me going.

As I keep flicking through the diary more entries talk about Maggie being unwell, going to the doctor and being signed off from work with stress and then I reach this entry.

4th July 1994

When I woke up this afternoon in the hospital, squinting through bleary eyes, my head felt like it could explode at any moment. Then I saw Mum pacing tight circles in the corner of the room. She was talking to herself and nodding, and I immediately felt guilty lying there in bed.

She looked across at me and smiled with relief whilst wrestling with her face not to be cross. I don't suppose you ever plan what to say when your daughter takes an overdose, the situation is new to us both. I am not sure if I wanted to survive or not, everything was too exhausting, daily life had become impossible and simply existing was taking more effort than I had left in my body.

The tablets didn't make me feel any better and I don't think it's only about Tom anymore, I am lonely, and I don't want this to be my life.

Mum said I was asleep for nearly two full days, and they said I was lucky to be alive when they brought me in, but I don't feel lucky.

I am shocked, I never knew that she took an overdose and unjustly strongly believe she should have told me.

Questions start whizzing around, is this why she wanted to come home from the hospital as soon as our sons were born?

Did she think they would find out and judge her ability to be a mother in some way, or that I would judge her for something that she had done years before we met?

I wonder if we all have secrets from the past that we don't share but most of us don't write them down so no one ever knows about them, they are safely stored within our vaults.

How well do I know her, how well do we know anyone?

I ponder the dilemma of talking about this with Maggie now. If I do bring it up, will it confuse and hurt her, probably, when she has hidden it from me for all these years?

I am not finding the happy memories I am searching for.

15th July 1994

I have resigned. I am not sure what I am going to do next, something needs to change. I don't want to stay in this flat with all the memories.

Every time I go out, I bump into someone we both know, and I try to avoid eye contact. I can't stand their looks of pity and discomfort as they struggle to know what to say to me, it is driving me mad. They know and I know Tom has got engaged again and has a baby on the way with the person he left me for, I am ready to escape from this place and these people.

I don't know who knows what about my hospital stay and I feel ashamed about it, I don't want to discuss it with these half-strangers or anyone ever again.

I felt empowered as soon as I made the decision to leave my school and the area. I am taking charge of my life instead of letting things happen to me and passively accepting them.

I am moving in with Mum and Dad which feels like a big step backwards, but it will give me some time to decide what to do next and I won't be under any financial pressure. Mum and I have always got on well although we haven't lived together for years so it will be interesting to see how it goes.

29th July 1994

When I walked across the grass this morning towards the front door of my childhood home, I could hear Dad shouting at me for not using the path as if it was only yesterday and I was returning home from school.

Entering my old bedroom was like stepping back in time, I became fifteen again, and it even smelled the same, like joss sticks mixed with my old Charlie perfume. The posters are still up, shrine-like in my absence, Queen and Culture Club feature equally and a selection of my old books are in the bookcase, I always loved reading to escape.

My wardrobe has some clothes in it from years ago waiting for my return, they will wait forever because that version of Maggie is long gone.

As I look down at the bed, I am pleased to see that at least the quilt cover has changed, and I am no longer sleeping under the two members of Wham.

30th July 1994

When I woke up this morning, my first morning back in my old single bed, it took me a moment to realise I was at Mum and Dad's not still dreaming.

On my bedside table was a cooling cup of tea in my old mug with Black Beauty on the front, some things never change. I contemplate my future as "You are a failure in every part of your life" chants repeatedly in my head.

More entries throughout the rest of the year with Maggie still off work and recovering from what I think was probably a breakdown.

I find it difficult to imagine her in this way, my Maggie is so strong.

21st January 1995

Nearly six months after moving in and I am starting to make plans to move out.

I drew a circle on a map around every place up to an hour away from Mum and Dad as I didn't want to go too far, and I've decided to head further south putting more distance between my old life and my new one.

Maybe the more miles I drive the better chance I have of my heart and mind mending, doubtful, but it's worth a try and I am actively looking for somewhere to live.

4th April 1995

Moving day and I have mixed feelings about moving out on my own again.

Mum has been brilliant at looking after me and I reverted to my dutiful daughter role while she enjoyed mothering me again. I am stronger than when I arrived and a stone heavier from all her puddings.

Dad was Dad, I know he would help me in a crisis, but he is still a bit belittling, questioning how I could give up such a good job. He has no understanding of how unwell I was, believing that getting on with things and not talking about anything is the best medicine. Mum knows how to play him though and protected me from his full force as she always has done.

So, I venture alone into a small rented terraced house on a backstreet in Oxford with a tidy back garden and spring bulbs beginning to flower, to make my new start in the world.

I have never lived in a house as old as this, I like the room sizes and know I will enjoy putting my own stamp on everything to make it feel like home. This time I can buy what I like, I don't have to compromise over the patterns I choose, and pink and purple can feature heavily if I want them to. The best thing is I don't have to have a TV taking up a whole wall.

When I start planning each room I am brimming with excitement and looking forward to things again, at last, I am enjoying being single.

I feel like I have survived a hurricane and this house is my safe haven.

5th June 1995

Buoyed by my success at moving house, my newfound independence, and my lack of long-term funds I've decided to join a teaching agency to try to get a position somewhere in Oxford supply teaching.

I presume the stress and pressure will be less than anything full-time, and I can turn things down if it gets too much, I am ready and surprised at how positive I feel.

26th June 1995

I have been offered a supply teaching job and I have said yes, and now I need to shop to look like a capable and responsible teacher again. My comfy tracksuits are not suitable, and my out-of-control hair needs attention, if I look like a teacher again, I will be a teacher, maybe!

The nerves are churning in my stomach, but they are normal. I keep having to convince myself that I am not overly anxious and stressed, they are only normal nerves, and everyone gets them it means I care.

4th July 1995

My first day at the new school involved taking lots of deep breaths, I had to keep telling myself I would survive with a class full of pupils and that I was capable of teaching again. Slowly convincing myself through the night that I was ready to go back, arguing for both sides in my mind.

If I hated it, I would be gone soon anyway or I could leave, I am only a supply teacher after all. I car danced to "Simply the Best" for motivation on the way into the school, headbanging along at the traffic lights as I tried to channel my inner Tina Turner until a sour-faced grey-haired lady pulled up next to me and pursed her lips in disapproval.

My positive mindset was firmly in place, and I got there with an hour to spare as I worried about the traffic and the parking to add to my long list of worries.

Walking in, the adrenaline carried me through the door and when the head teacher barked "Classroom Two, left onto the corridor with the green floor markings, second door on the right" it felt fantastically familiar. I had made it, and standing in the doorway of the classroom I wondered how bad a class of A-level students could be.

I cannot believe I was so nervous today, everyone was lovely, the teachers were relieved to have some help and the students wanted to be there.

One student Mike was intense and held my gaze like someone older would, I was not sure what to make of him. I have three more days booked for this week, I am covering absence due to sickness apparently, but no one seems to know for how long. I am going to be grateful for something every day to remind myself of all the good things that can happen, then I can look back at them for reassurance when I think everything is against me or if things start to fall apart.

Today I am grateful because…
I am a teacher and I made it through day one.

7th July 1995

The sickness turns out to be a hysterectomy so I will be here covering for the absent teacher for a while longer, yippee! I like the school but am sorry for the teacher obviously!

Today I am grateful because…
I am getting paid again.

21st July 1995

It is the last day of term, and I wish it wasn't I am enjoying the routine of work. Mike stayed behind after class, it's not like he's 17 at all. He offered to show me around Oxford, and I don't know anyone here, I am sure that's okay, isn't it?

He seems genuine and kind and it will be great to have something to look forward to this summer.

Today I am grateful because…
Mike is becoming my friend.

I can't explain how strange it is to read about yourself in your now-wife's diary, getting an insight all these years later into how she felt when we first met.

A snapshot in time of what it was like for Maggie, it's confusing to read our developing love story and remember it clearly when I am swamped with thoughts of how Maggie is today.

5th August 1995

Met Mike for a coffee, he's good company, interesting, funny, and thoughtful.

I am surprised we had so much to talk about, he seems older and more serious than me in some ways. We are meeting again next weekend at a pub out of town with live music. I questioned if he should be at the pub at 17 and he looked at me like I was mad and said they have all been going since they were 15. I am not his parents after all, and it is just for a few drinks.

Today I am grateful because…

I live in Oxford, and I am bravely going out into the world again.

11th August 1995

It turned out to be a Rainbow tribute band and Mike hadn't heard of the band the first time they were around. So, while I was at the school disco, aged about 13 dancing about hoping to be noticed in my rah-rah skirt in 1983, he probably hadn't even started school, now I feel old!

We both drank cider and the more I drank the more I sang. The chip van on the way home made me smile it's years since I had chips after a night out, I forgot I was in Oxford when I ordered gravy with my chips, no chance this far south!

Today I am grateful because…

My life is becoming more fun again.

19th August 1995

Mike and I met for lunch at a quiet country pub on the outskirts of town and he tried to kiss me and we sort of kissed. I feel like a teenager again, no one saw us, I don't know what to do. It's mad!

How can I like a 17-year-old, I am 25. Am I his Mrs Jones moment?

It doesn't feel that way though, we have talked about everything, and it didn't feel odd or wrong, but is it?

I can't sleep, I feel sick, have I crossed a line I can't get back over, and what about my job, he is a pupil. I need to speak to Mike.

Today I am grateful because…

I can't answer this today, the thoughts in my head are too frightening to acknowledge.

20th August 1995

Met Mike for a coffee and feel a bit better, think the croissant helped after not eating last night.

I have made it clear whatever this is, it must wait until he's 18 to go any further and until I won't be teaching him. I am so mixed up, I like him and I know for sure he likes me. I need to be the adult in this situation, but Mike is calmer and more in control than me. I am irresponsible and will not let anything else happen.

Today I am grateful because…

I can still have these types of feelings after what happened with Tom, but I wish Mike was older.

Various entries about our developing relationship trigger the happiest of memories.

We spent so much time together all through that first summer. I showed her Oxford as a tour guide would, but I had to learn it first to make myself sound knowledgeable and interesting. I was regularly cramming in facts, I had never done so much work in the holidays.

We got together about 6 months after the summer, our dating was quite old-fashioned mainly because Maggie wanted to take it slowly, now I understand why.

Maggie got a permanent job at another school about a year later and was happy. I had forgotten the details that she had written down about the following few years. The places we went, the bands we saw, nervously going on holiday abroad and her nerves when I was finally meeting her parents for the first time.

Reading about our perfect life emphasises how much I have already lost. I stop next at an entry from the day before we got married in January 1998.

23rd January 1998

I will never understand how the universe and fate collided and landed me at a school in Oxford, then chose a pupil to become the love of my life. He knew from the start that I was the one and we would be together forever, he is kinder, wiser, smarter, and less complicated than me, as well as being my best friend.

I cannot comprehend how much I love him, when people talked about soulmates I never understood until Mike. In Four Weddings and a Funeral when one of the characters says "he is my north, my south, my east, my west" Mike is that, he is everything to me, I can never imagine my life without him.

I am getting married tomorrow and need to sleep which is never going to happen, I am far too excited. I can sleep tomorrow night when we are together and I am back in his arms, and he will be my husband and I will be his wife, Mrs Maggie Trafford.

I have practised my new signature lots of times, as we did at Junior school when we thought we would marry our favourite boy from the class. Back then getting married and having children seemed so easy through my child's eyes, I am grateful that I had the innocence of not knowing the reality of how challenging it would be to get to this part of my life.

She is the love of my life; how can I continue my life without her in it?

Maggie accepted me from the beginning, never asking me for anything but my true self. I can't believe I am reading her inner thoughts. I want to go back to that time, start over again and re-live it, changing nothing except her illness. How many people can say they want exactly the same life over again?

This time I know I would stop to appreciate everything, not take it for granted or moan about the things that didn't go quite right. Her illness puts everything into perspective, I've wasted time worrying about things that didn't happen. Now, I can't help her with the bloody big thing that she has to face and I can't fix it, everything seems meaningless.

I notice I am smudging the ink with my tears, that's enough of the diaries for today.

As I look around at some of the other boxes, Maggie has marked some "Mum's stuff" I don't know what to do with them, should I keep them forever or see if Maggie can help me sort them out?

It was so difficult when Maggie's mum died suddenly, it was a shock for everyone. Cancer destroyed her, eating its way through her whole body, it was only three months from diagnosis to death.

Dan and Sam were close to their gran and spent time over there in the holidays. They never became the grandchildren Maggie's dad would have liked, the boy's interests didn't measure up to his narrow view of what a boy's activities should be, exclusively including rugby, football, and cricket.

Maggie and I wanted them to experience a wide variety of sports, cultures, people and places so they could make up their minds about the world and decide for themselves how they wanted to live their lives.

We once spent an uncomfortable lunch at a local restaurant for Maggie's dad's birthday after her mum's cancer diagnosis, where he informed us loudly what we were doing wrong in the way we were bringing up our children. Maggie's mum was too weak to pacify him and defend anyone and Maggie and I let it go over our heads as he ranted on, thoroughly enjoying the sound of his own voice, getting louder the more he drank.

Maggie's dad moved on within a year mentally and physically, he moved in with the lady who owned the local café before they decided to move to Spain.

For a man who spent years resisting any change, who never agreed to holidays abroad, with his obnoxious fixed opinions that he freely shared with us, we struggled to understand his sudden personality transplant.

Ironically, he took great pride in telling Maggie that life is too short after her mum died, and on the day we moved nearer to my parents he was boarding an easyJet flight to Spain.

2016 - Maisy

Over the next few months Jody and I speak all the time as well as constantly texting each other, her messages are full of emoji hearts, ponies, smiley faces, and flowers which let me know she's okay. She likes her new house, it's a rented one, but they might buy it if it comes up for sale.

It's near horse-riding stables and she had her first lesson last week and loved it, she will have a pony next no doubt. She is still swimming and has joined a new swim team and is practising for next season's races, she says she is making friends but it's not like we are friends who know everything about each other.

Her mum is busy making the house feel like home, more grey paint I imagine, and her dad's job is working out well. The best news is that she has got an apprenticeship at the local vet which runs alongside her college course.

It's her dream job to work with animals, it's not great money to start with but she doesn't care. She says her mum says I can come and stay when they are more sorted, I am so happy it's working out for her.

She doesn't ask about Shaun, and I don't mention him, I miss seeing her, but we will meet up soon.

2016 - Sam

Before the mum news, we had all been planning to meet up at school on GCSE results day, loads of us, to get our results together.

We were going to go out and celebrate or commiserate with each other. I'm not going, I can't face seeing everyone, they all know about Mum. No one knows what to say and I don't need my whole year looking at me, pity and sympathy are the worst.

Some of our mates are leaving school for good, not staying for the sixth form, I might not see them again. I didn't realise that mattered to me until now, too much change at the same time is hard to think about.

I did better than I thought I would, Maisy did well too and she's spoken to Jody and her results will get her where she wants to be. Shaun, of course, did brilliantly he's second in the whole school, a real poster boy, and the teachers love him. I wasted my day, my moment to celebrate, by feeling sorry for myself, I couldn't shake off the tangled web of anxiety about what would happen to our family next.

The week before Christmas, Dad goes into school to see my head of year, Mr Johnson, to let him know about Mum. Mr Johnson has always had too much skin, a baggy face with folds of skin that will never fill out, and now when he looks at me across the classroom with his sad kind brown eyes he reminds me of a rescue dog, maybe a bulldog, looking through the bars of his cage waiting, hoping to be chosen.

He doesn't know what to say to me and I always put my head down not wanting to make eye contact as he looks across the class. Dad said the school will support me with anything I need, whatever that means.

Why Dad thinks he needed to tell them I don't know, I wish he hadn't, I can't escape at school without all the teachers looking at me, pitying my situation, it makes me stand out. I don't need everyone in school talking about me and pointing at the boy with the mad mum.

Dan is home for Christmas, he never normally comes into my room. It's not as if we don't get on, we do, but we like our own space and Dan never talks to me about anything, he seems to just get on with things. So, when he came into my room and sat on the corner of my bed, I probably looked confused because we've never been those sorts of brothers.

He said he was worried about Dad as he wasn't eating and had lost weight. Would I be able to keep an eye on him when he goes back to uni? He will come back as often as he can, but he can't be here all the time to help Dad out with Mum he says, "Dad needs help and he won't ask you, you need to offer."

Haven't I been helping?

Do things go on around me that I don't notice, am I so wrapped up in my life I've not thought about Dad? I'm angry with Dan, blaming him for leaving "Why don't you stay if you're so bothered?" I shout, how can he accuse me of not helping?

Is he right, do I need to grow up?

My life has carried on almost as normal because I've made sure I'm not here, so everything has changed, but not for me. I've avoided being here, spending more and more time at Shaun's in our fantasy game world where I don't have to think, and escaping to Maisy's where I don't have to talk, she talks enough for both of us.

This way I can pretend everything at home is normal as I'm not here to witness the destruction and carnage of my old life as the bomb explodes, I figured I don't need to be here to see it.

How dare Dan accuse me of not helping, does he think I don't care, does Dad think that? Dan left, not me, he should stay here with us if he's so worried. I'm shouting at him now, telling him to leave me alone, inside it's like a volcano, always ready to explode, just below the surface in my chest pushing up into my throat. I need to push it down all the time so it doesn't come out through my mouth, my nose, or my eyes because if it starts, I might never be able to stop it.

Dan twists his mouth, breathes deeply, and gives a sad shrug, gestures all more painful to me than if he were shouting. I've not seen him cry since I was about six and he was eight when he accidentally dropped his Nintendo DS into the sea off Whitby Pier. Time froze at that moment and we both stood still as the wind and rain battered us while Mum tried her best not to be too cross because it was an accident.

I know he's disappointed in me, he thought I was more grown up and he came to talk to me to ask for help. He looks straight into my eyes from the doorway before he leaves, for what seems like ages, with neither of us willing to look away. I won't look away; I silently challenge him to continue, to dare to say more, defiantly holding his gaze. He bites his bottom lip which he always does when he's anxious and looks teary when he quietly shuts my door.

The silence after my shouting speaks volumes giving me plenty of time to reflect on what a crap son I am and how much I hate my brother for making me feel like this. Just because he's older doesn't mean he's right.

Deep inside I know he's right and asking for help, the knot in the pit of my stomach is starting to untie itself, I need to retie it tighter this time, make the ends secure so I can keep moving forward, not thinking, barely existing.

I can't keep going over it, I need to move forward and try to help Dad more, then talk to Dan and sort things out, we never fall out.

I am turning into someone I don't recognise and I don't like him.

2017 - Sam

The row with Dan was the turning point for me, it was what I needed to hear, you can rely on your brother to let you know when you aren't pulling your weight, and I couldn't carry on acting the way I had been.

Dan and I arranged a huge bouquet of flowers for Mother's Day. We never bothered that much before, if we had known what was going to happen, we might have made more of an effort.

Mum seems to understand they are for her and hugs the delivery man tightly when the flowers arrive, she thinks they are from him, and invites him in for a drink. That's another thing Dad and I are trying to get used to, she looks completely normal, but you have to mop up around her more and more explaining to startled strangers what's going on.

She did it in the local shop a few weeks ago when Dad was with her, she had a basket full of shopping and just walked out. One of the staff darted round from behind the counter shouting after her, as Dad raced down from the other end of the shop and out of the door to catch her.

They brought her back inside and Dad tried to explain to the sceptical staff about Mum. Mum was very cross and made lots of hand gestures he didn't know she knew as she kept repeating "There is nothing wrong with me!" which didn't help.

It's Maisy's 17th birthday today and I want to try to make her feel special, I tell her it's her choice, we can do whatever she wants, and I don't mind what we do or where we go.

In the end, she decides to go bowling and Shaun comes too. It's weird doing familiar things when what is going on in my head is so different to the last time I was here. I surprise myself though and take pleasure from launching the balls at the pins. It's a chance to escape and hit something without causing any damage.

I bought her a silver bracelet and had it engraved with Maisy on one side and Sam on the other. I thought she was going to cry when I gave it to her, she said it was the best gift I had ever given her, so at least I got something right.

It's 5am when I sit bolt upright on my 17th birthday and hear "Walking on Sunshine" playing downstairs at full volume. Dad and I meet on the landing and rush downstairs to find Mum shouting along as I turn it off.

She is looking for the house keys and pacing up and down the hall from the front door to the back, trying the door handles over and over again. She is dressed in a short pink nightshirt with her bomber jacket over the top and her penguin slippers on.

When she looks at us, she freezes, and puts her hands up in front of her face, in a gesture where it looks like she is trying to hide, tell us to stop and not come any closer all at the same time.

It takes Dad over an hour to convince her to go back to bed. I put the kettle on, refill the tea caddy and wonder what sort of conversations we will have over these new teabags. Dad comes to join me and we sit in the silence of our thoughts at the kitchen table.

I got some money from Mum and Dad for my birthday which I will need if I want to start driving, everyone I know is learning to drive and some have passed their test already. I don't have the headspace to think about it, there's enough going on, maybe I will do it next year.

Mum is getting worse; her symptoms are speeding up and the confusion on her face is there every day as she struggles to remember who we are and who she is. She did have a lucid moment today and made raspberry jelly and ice cream for me which we all ate at the table in suspended silence, holding our breath between each spoonful willing ourselves to get through it without incident, she hasn't made jelly since I was about ten.

The rest of my birthday passed by without further celebration at home, Dad tried to make a fuss, but we all remembered last year, my 16th, some of us better than others.

In the end, Maisy convinced me to go and see a film at night, so we went to see King Arthur, Legend of the Sword, it was worth the effort, I slept better in the cinema seat than I'd slept in my bed for months. Maisy talked animatedly about the film all the way back and I nodded along agreeably feeling more like the old me.

2017 - Mike

I am not sure when I first consciously acknowledged that I had started to physically fight with Maggie to protect her from herself, or when I realised that acknowledging this horrible stage and accepting it were two different things.

I know it's getting out of hand, our regular fights happen at least once a week which is frightening and it can't carry on. Today we fought because I wouldn't give her the car keys or let her out of the house to go to the bus stop and ride to the park on her own.

She doesn't understand the danger, and she has no comprehension or warning system left to help her process what could go wrong. I can't explain it to her because it's not Maggie standing there, physically it's her, mentally we are arguing as we did with Dan and Sam when they were toddlers.

It always ends the same way with Maggie shouting and swearing at me, trampling over my feelings completely unaware that she is doing this. Slamming doors and shutting herself in our bedroom, it's like having another child in the house, except this time one that will never grow up.

It's getting worse, as Maggie gets more confused and can't work out who we are and why we are in the house with her. Sometimes she looks frightened and shakes, lips trembling like she thinks we might hurt her.

We sit down when this happens to look less threatening, we are all a foot taller than she is so we sit and watch her fold into herself, yoga-like, trying to make herself disappear, it's what a child does when they cover their eyes thinking they can't see you so you can't see them.

No words can describe how it makes me feel for Maggie to be thinking I could ever hurt her.

She thinks I am her dad today which is depressing because she wasn't close to her dad, and he could be cruel and manipulative to get his own way with Maggie and her mum.

I am trying to get her into the car for her first overnight stay at Greenacres, the nursing home. My neck is tense, and my shoulders ache and rise towards my ears, physically I couldn't be more uncomfortable, relax, relax, relax, I repeat to myself through clamped teeth.

Maggie senses my tension and knows something is wrong but not what. She takes her cues from me, like young children do with adults in stressful situations. I repeat out loud calm, calm, and breathe, as if this is something we do every day.

I look across at the ticking clock on the mantlepiece and try to time my breathing with every five ticks as the hand moves around, while looking out through the French doors at the garden imagining our life before this.

It is the sort of day when we would have been out in the garden from early morning until late at night, sunbathing, chatting, reading, and relaxing with a good bottle of wine or two. The boys would have joined us for a BBQ later, maybe with friends. That's other people's lives now.

When we get to Greenacres everyone, including Maggie, is all smiles like she is greeting long-lost friends, it makes it easier for me to leave her there and drive away.

She doesn't know where she is she thinks it is some sort of holiday, and I am not going to correct her. It is still only 11am and I don't pick her up until tomorrow morning, I have no idea what to do with my day.

Free time is an alien concept to me, trying to give enough to everyone at work, to Maggie and the boys as well as feeding us, keeping the house in some sort of order and going to the doctors and hospital appointments, it doesn't leave much time for what I want to do.

I decide to clean the house thoroughly for the first time in ages, and part way through wonder why anyone would choose to be a cleaner. However, it is mildly cathartic to be cleaning and organising everything, until I panic and worry that I have moved too many things and Maggie won't like it, so I retrace my steps and move everything back to where it was.

Dan and Sam appear mid-afternoon, not knowing what to say but realising they should probably be here which makes me think we did something right bringing them up, and we all head to the pub for tea.

It is difficult to articulate how massive the Maggie-shaped hole is, as we sit quietly looking at the menu and the empty chair. It's not only her physical presence but also the way she could start a conversation and knew how to involve us all, and the way she could easily get the boys to speak and use more than a one-syllable answer.

I underestimated the simple joy of having the people you love most in the world sitting together at a table, and I never expected a part of my heart to be sitting at a different table in a nursing home right now.

2017 - Cassie

"Cassie Wilson from 6H, expelled!" are the first words Mike says to me after over 20 years when I pass him on the corridor at Greenacres.

I am not proud of it, being expelled, I was a mixed-up kid from a chaotic background and showing off was my armour. Times have changed for me since then, I have been working as a counsellor for over ten years now, and life has moved on, he hasn't changed much though.

We always wanted the boys from the year above to like us, we thought they were more sophisticated than the ones in our year. Mike was the moody quiet type, well into his music and quite a few of us tried to get his attention back then.

We couldn't believe it when we found out he was dating our English teacher, Miss Wright, we all liked her, she made the lessons fun and she was one of the few that cared if we understood the work, she wanted us to do well. I think a lot of the boys fancied her and were jealous of what happened. Mike was always more grown up than the rest of us, I didn't know they were still together, had two children and made a go of it, until today.

When I ask him who he is visiting I am shocked to learn that it is Miss Wright, well Mrs Trafford otherwise known as Maggie his wife.

I follow Mike back down the corridor to meet her and wonder if I should mention to Mike that I met Maggie when she first chose Greenacres as her forever home. I am trying to work out how old she will be now as I walk.

She is sitting in the corner chair in the sunny lounge when we walk in, fidgeting, concentrating on rolling her fingers rapidly over each other, I can see she is agitated, she is probably trying to work out where she is.

It's not difficult to recognise her now I see them together, they both look almost the same as they did at school, except they have different hairstyles and Mike looks older than she does. This stage of Alzheimer's is always challenging for everyone, some things still seem familiar, but they can't work out why, and other things pop into their mind like they happened yesterday, but in reality, they happened years ago.

I have seen it with almost all of the residents when they first start to visit. The families often say it was the worst time for them, offering false hope, getting glimpses of their loved one appearing completely normal until they remember what is happening to them and they become increasingly distressed and frightened.

It is hard to comfort someone, resident or relative when there is no getting better.

When Maggie looks up at me, I think I see a flicker of recognition as Mike introduces me and mentions our school, I don't embellish my colourful past, it's not about me, I am here to help Maggie.

I will need to speak to the family more soon to understand what is normal for Maggie, how quiet or outgoing she usually is, how she shows signs of heightened distress and what type of activities she likes to do so we can settle her in quickly.

Hundreds of questions will help me to understand more about her life, and once she starts visiting Greenacres regularly it will become more of a routine and easier for everyone, the first few visits are always a struggle. I know from experience if Maggie can settle and feel safe with us, her family will feel less guilty and have a chance at making a life for themselves when she eventually moves in.

It's so sad for them all, she will be our youngest resident, nobody expects this to happen, how can you prepare your children for this?

As I move towards the door to leave them alone Maggie shouts at Mike, telling him to get his hands off her as he tries to persuade her it's time to go. I can see how uncomfortable he is, he looks embarrassed not knowing what to say or do. He is gently trying to manoeuvre her towards reception and out into the car to take her home.

I step in and Maggie transforms into a chatty, smiley giggly girl in front of our eyes. He mouths thank you across the car park and shrugs, I know it hurts him deeply that his wife doesn't want to go home with him.

A few weeks later and Mike has asked me to go for a coffee with him to talk about how Maggie is getting on when she visits. I'm feeling a bit nervous, I wouldn't normally meet a resident's husband outside of work, but he has asked me, and I can't find a good reason to say no, after all, I have known him for years so why wouldn't I go?

I get there first and when Mike arrives, he gets out his computer, opens a huge spreadsheet and asks about Maggie's care, payment plans, bringing in flowers and lots of other things that have been keeping him awake at night.

It's obvious he needs to talk to someone, I think he is so busy worrying about everyone else, that he isn't looking after himself. I don't say anything, I don't want to pry and cross over any professional boundary, but the pain is written all over his face, and he keeps wringing his hands and breathing out in short loud breaths, clearly trying to keep control of his emotions but needing to let the pressure escape somehow.

After the question-and-answer session, we talk about our old school and all the people we knew, with me updating him on where people are now, and he asks about my life. I tell him about my family, what my sisters are doing and all about my nieces, and when he asks about my personal life and if I have a partner or a husband, I tell him about my disastrous dating history over the last few years. How it consists of a string of hopeless dates after using a couple of dating apps, and that I am not using the app where sex is expected on the first date, I would like to get to know someone more first please, I don't think that's too much to ask, is it?

I don't know why I feel the need to mention this, and immediately feel stupid when the words are out of my mouth. To his credit, Mike nods as I chatter on and explain I'm not expecting to find anyone but I'm not giving up either, I don't want to be on my own forever.

I carry on filling any gaps in the conversation talking about anything and everything. We are there for nearly two hours, and as I drive home, I go over the conversations again, examining what I said in forensic detail, despairing at myself for some of the things I disclosed.

I think about what a good man Mike is, how his life has been devastated, and the pain that is still to come, anyone can see how much he loves his family.

2017 - *Sam*

I am thinking to myself we are going on a day trip to the seaside to avoid the horror of what is actually going on. But my mind keeps connecting me with regular reminders that today I am going to see the place where we are going to send Mum away to forever, eventually.

I can't understand how it's the right thing to do. Mum and Dad have been to visit the home many times, and Dad keeps telling me how right it is for Mum, I think he is trying to convince us both.

Rationally, I know Dad can't cope and things are getting worse, and I understand he will need a life of his own one day. But I keep thinking, would Mum do the same if it was the other way round, and if something bad had happened to me or Dan would she have ever sent us away?

Mum's face is full of childlike expressions a lot of the time, she's an actor over-exaggerating everything, playing to the audience. Happy looks like the best day of her life while her sad face is heart-breaking. I need to leave the room every time she begins to cry, I can't handle it even now nearly two years later, I can't get used to the wide eyes, face crumpling and childlike sobs, she's not my mum anymore.

I know she is, but I don't want her to be. "Extremes of expression" the experts call it, I try not to be embarrassed by her if we are out but it's hard and I wish I didn't feel like this. Everyone else's mum is normal, mine can't remember who I am. I know I sound selfish but it's not fair and I am angry, I felt better for a while but she's getting much worse, and I can't get past being cross with everyone. I hardly shouted before the Alzheimer's diagnosis, but I can't stop shouting now.

After all my worrying, taking Mum into Greenacres wasn't that bad, Mum was excited to be there and seemed to remember being there before and it was only a visit this time.

On the way home I decide that I want to go back to being a child, back to the age when I was standing in the kitchen fighting with Dan over the skin on top of the custard. When the biggest thing I had to worry about was what was for tea, hoping it wasn't Monday when it was always cold meat left over from Sunday Dinner.

I realise I've had a protected childhood with no big problems. I've never had to worry about money like Shaun worries with his mum or think about my sister all the time as Maisy does. My life was easy before this, it's my turn now. Maybe we all take turns passing around the hot potato hoping the music doesn't stop when we are holding it, changing our lives, and making them unrecognisable.

Dad introduced me to Cassie while we were at Greenacres, he thinks it would be good if I talk to her, she is some sort of counsellor who visits homes in the area and works with residents and their families. I have agreed to book some time with her on my next visit, I don't know what good it will do, Dad looked so hopeful I couldn't say no.

The next time Mum goes into Greenacres I meet with Cassie, and she says it could help to think about what is happening to Mum the way you would think about a death without the funeral. Meaning, that the person

I knew and loved as my mum is not there, it's not my mum inside her anymore, she has gone, and the disease has taken over.

This is true, it's more confusing because she looks almost the same as before, if you didn't know her well, you would say she looks the same. Apparently, there are stages of grief people go through and it's not surprising I've been angry, it is normal, expected, and an essential part of moving forward.

Talking it through and opening myself up to someone not connected to our family is a relief, Dad was right.

When Cassie says "Your mum would want you to be happy again" it makes me think, and I have to bite my lip hard and clench my fists, so I don't cry.

She explains that Mum is happy in her own way, her mind is in another place, but she's not in pain and has started to make friends when she visits. She looks forward to coming and will settle in well when she's here full-time, she joins in and loves painting in the art classes.

Fairness doesn't come into it according to Cassie, it's not fair for the family she says, some people stay stuck in that place forever, the "why me" sort of people. Cassie says people have to move on from thinking that, nobody knows why things happen and she doesn't have all the answers, but caring for those who are suffering is more productive than self-indulgent sulking in her book, and hanging onto the past doesn't change anything.

She says it's easier when the residents don't remember the past at all, they accept life again somehow. A new other life they didn't want, but it's better than the confusion, she's watched the pain they go through when they are trying to remember, a revolving door of memories getting faster and faster, memories they can't slow down and reach anymore. I try to imagine everything I know slowly slipping away from me, remembering less and less, and I picture reaching out my fingertips to touch something familiar, my family, as they move further and further away from me.

I conclude that Cassie is okay, very matter-of-fact not warm like Mum, no bullshit either, and none of the talk I hate about things happening for a reason thank God, so that's good.

I will see her again, it's easier than trying to talk to Dad, he can't talk to anyone, he's so quiet and lost and shut down, wrestling with himself about sending Mum away, he needs to talk to someone too.

2017 - Maisy

Anna and Mum are not well so I need to be at home. I hate taking time off school, I am finding my A-levels difficult, and I will need to catch up with the work I miss today and add it to the other work I am already behind on.

Sometimes I have no choice, they can't cope without me; it's happening more and more but I can't just walk out the door and leave them. Mum is trying to get some extra help but it's not easy to find and it's expensive. I know she doesn't want me to miss school, she wants me to go to university and have a chance to be whatever I want to be, right now I can't see that happening.

A week after my latest unplanned day off I meet Dad at the soulless coffee shop tucked behind the bridge in town.

Dad chooses it because they serve proper portions, not like all the chain ones he says with all the fancy teas and plastic sandwiches and two bites of cake costing a fortune. When you walk into this café you know they serve chips, and when you walk out you smell like you've been cooking them.

My hair smells horrible every time we leave here, and the smell stays on your clothes, it sinks in somehow and everything has to go straight into the wash when I get home. Anyway, I don't mind today because I haven't seen Dad for ages, he's been working away for nearly a year.

After we order he asks about my A levels, I shrug, and he looks closely at me questioning my face, and before he says anything else, I burst into tears. It all comes out; how exhausted Mum is and how she's not coping, so I am at home too much helping with Anna.

I feel disloyal to Mum, as soon as I stop talking, so I move on quickly to talk about Sam, I explain how I am trying to help and support him with his mum. I mention Jody leaving so suddenly and what happened to her, and I tell Dad how I miss having Jody to talk to.

I am also trying to say how much I have missed him being around without saying the words, I don't want to make him feel guilty, it's tiring enough carrying Mum's guilt around.

Instead of being cross, which I thought he would be about the missing school part, he listens and nods slowly looking concerned, then he hands me his ironed handkerchief, which makes me smile. Whatever Dad is wearing even if it's a tracksuit he always has a clean ironed handkerchief in his pocket. It's such a clear memory from always being his little sunshine girl, and it takes me back to all my cut knees when I was learning to ride a bike, and the worst time ever when he left us, he always gave me his handkerchief.

He reaches across the table and puts his hand on top of mine, holding onto my life with his hand, smiling with understanding, while holding tightly onto his tea with his other hand. The reality of the last year and all that has happened to me continues to tumble clumsily out.

As I look across at the other tables after my spectacularly noisy sobbing episode, I think thank goodness no one I know would be seen dead in here and I openly continue to cry into my hot chocolate.

Dad doesn't care if I cry and wail and every table notices, he never worries about what other people think, he says he hasn't got the time or energy to try and keep everyone else happy because you end up being unhappy yourself, and please no one in the end.

I don't want him to have a go at Mum later though, so I make sure he knows she hasn't asked me to stay at home to look after them, I make it clear it was my decision.

By the time my bacon sandwich arrives, I have pulled myself together and Dad is talking about the responsibility for everything not being mine and getting some help for Mum, he mentions calling around more and paying for some proper care at home for Anna.

Secretly I know it's too late for my mock exams I have failed them, trying to revise at home was impossible with constant chaos and nowhere peaceful to work. Sitting at school and looking at everyone scribbling away in the massive exam hall was painful and handing in my papers with lots of blank spaces, it's not hard to figure out I've failed.

I know I can pass if I have some time and space to study, I want to do well, and it would give me a chance to study before the real thing, and I might still be able to get into uni.

When Dad and I got back to my house I thought convincing Mum would be the hardest part of the plan, having someone else coming into our home is basically saying she can't cope with her own daughter, but Mum is exhausted and doesn't object.

Mum and Dad sit in the kitchen with me as though I am another adult, and we talk through another version of our life going forward, I am even allowed a glass of wine as we toast our new plan.

I can remember them being together when they talk this way, joking about me with shiny eyes and secret smiles both proud of the daughter they have created. Dad is true to his word and within a week help has arrived and Dad is paying.

Help comes in the form of the efficient Ruth, a large slightly scary lady with the loudest deepest laugh I have ever heard, she makes Anna laugh loads. Her family are all grown up and she wants to help look after ours she tells us, adding that we look like we could do with her help more than once.

We all like her though, and adjust to her being there comfortably, we are happy to let her take charge and magically mould around her as we realise how much we need this change. We call her Mary, which makes her laugh, after Mary Poppins, although she looks nothing like the film version her impact is the same.

Ruth must have been a great mum, she knows what each of us needs and our home is less of a pressure cooker, the jokes are coming back, and Mum and I are starting to take things less personally.

Dad is calling in at least twice a week and is even staying for tea every Wednesday, which is a bit weird, but Anna loves him being there pulling his silly faces, I am not sure he will ever grow up.

Part 3

"New Beginnings" 2018

2018 - Mike

Maggie follows me through the back door as I go to put the bins out, Mrs Stewart from next door is doing her bins at the same time. She smiles across at us with an over-happy smile, the bright one you use when you are delivering bad news to your children.

I wish she wasn't smiling; I don't want to have to think about how she feels too, they were really friendly neighbours before this, they've lived there for over 40 years.

What's happening to Maggie is not like breaking your leg when people still want to visit you and you eventually recover. I don't think Mrs Stewart can deal with the way Maggie is now, maybe the window into this type of future is too close to home for her, fear does funny things to people.

As I open the side gate to negotiate the bins towards the front drive, Maggie makes a run for it, straight past me and out into the street. She looks determined and she is fast, turning left out of the drive, heading towards the park with me in hot pursuit, Tom and Jerry action live on our street.

She always turns left; I know she is trying to get to the park, and I will catch up with her soon, it always happens this way. When I reach her, we will have a big scene, with Maggie shouting and hissing and it will look as if I am taking her against her will, which technically I am.

Passing cars have been known to slow down about now, as the driver and passengers watch the action unfold and decide if they should get involved. Then her tears will start to fall as she can't understand why she can't go to the park today, and I will drag her home trying not to hurt her to get her inside before I lock our cage door for another day.

Except, it's hospital day today, so we need to move quickly when we get home to make the appointment on time.

Maggie is compliant when I put her coat on and get her in the car, and upbeat when we walk into the consultant's room for more tests, her very brightest smile is reserved for him.

As we walk into the same room I have been in many times, I reflect on the long journey we have been on to get to this point. It's not long in the average lifespan, but it feels like our whole lives have been consumed by this disease even before it was evident how strongly it was taking hold.

Talking endlessly and crying at the injustice in the beginning, then tentatively moving on to planning our future apart. I'm starting to forget our life before this. I am exhausted and the weight of responsibility pushes my body further into the ground it feels like I am stuck, trapped in a vice or like a captured animal, unable to escape its inevitable fate.

I can't understand any of it, I live life reacting to things that happen. I can't plan anything, Alzheimer's has a plan of its own and it's all-consuming, sucking the life out of me as well as Maggie.

I know what Maggie wanted to happen now, she was clear, I agreed reluctantly at the time not knowing what dealing with any of this would be like, but she knew. She had spent months researching likely outcomes and the speed of the disease, what caring for her would involve and ultimately, she chose us over her.

She was definite about what she wanted, and I agreed, when it's not happening it's abstract and you kid yourself it's still a long way off until you can't cope any longer and you are sitting alone in the place you dreaded reaching.

We still have lots of things to tick off our bucket list, so I never pictured this day, not yet. I nod as the consultant delivers his verdict, he's a crown court judge delivering our life sentence.

Maggie doesn't understand what he is saying she is playing with a wooden elephant on his desk. And so, we come to the decision that only I can make, and I know it is time to plan for Maggie to move to Green-acres forever.

The guilt of that thought doesn't hit me until later when I realise some of the guilt is tinged with relief, knowing I can't cope alone for much longer.

When I go into my mum's kitchen a thousand childhood memories walk in there with me.

I find Mum crying, so I know it has finally sunk in, Maggie is never getting better, and we need to move her to Greenacres soon. Mum spent a long time not believing the diagnosis, she never trusts what doctors say, and she kept saying Maggie was too young and they must have got it wrong.

I cry too, and it reminds me of being a small boy standing there needing a big hug. Mum has always been great at those, holding on tight until my tears stopped, putting down whatever she was doing to make me feel like the most important person in her world and finding a biscuit or a piece of cake to make it better.

The last time I cried in this kitchen our cat had been run over, I was nine years old, and I thought I would never stop crying, Mum was crying too. We all loved that cat, even Dad was sad, we could hear him sniffing from behind his paper. He dug a hole, and we had a sad little ceremony and buried her with her favourite mouse toy in the back garden, she is still there as far as I know.

It was always me and Mum in the kitchen, this is where she taught me to cook, and the table doubled as my homework desk. Dad never helped with anything domestic, because he didn't know how, it is a traditional marriage with old-fashioned roles and opinions in a lot of ways.

As I look around the room not much has changed, the same wallpaper is still up with outlines of abstract squares on it. The ones I coloured in with bright pencils are still there under the table, where I used to hide, imagining I was a spy who couldn't be seen, carrying out some important secret mission to save the world.

It's a small kitchen by today's standards, I never noticed how small when I was young, it suited the three of us, and I am a giant in it now.

Our house always smelt of furniture polish. When I was growing up Mum dusted every single day, I love the fact it still smells and looks the same.

We had proper food as Mum calls it, meat potatoes and two vegetables and we always had a pudding. We ate together at the table, always cremated beef for Sunday Dinner, nothing pink or still bleeding reached our plates, and fish was served without fail every Friday. On Mondays I tried to go to my mates for tea to escape the cold meat, I enjoy cold meat now, and the rest of us do apart from Sam, who tries to escape like I did.

If I went to Alan's house two doors down it was usually crispy pancakes, potato waffles and a fried egg served with sliced bread, the sort of tea we never had at home. I thought it was a fantastic tea at Alan's back then, and they had cold rice pudding straight out of a tin, I was shocked. Until I went there, I thought all puddings except ice cream and yoghurt were meant to be hot.

You think all parents must be the same when you are growing up, but then you get older and realise you all have your own individual family rulebook.

Mum and Dad love Maggie, and it's hard for them too. After a bumpy patch early in their relationship Mum often says what a great mother Maggie is, always putting the boys first, making them eat proper meals, such well-mannered and loving grandsons.

"We are so proud of you all," she writes in her card every Christmas.

When Mum speaks and says she is so sorry for me and the boys, it is the hardest thing to hear, I want to comfort her and she wants to comfort me, neither of us is equipped to talk about this.

2018 - Sam

Phoning Dan was a good decision, he's coming home this weekend to talk to Dad. I can't look after him on my own, he's not alright, he looks old and tired and has big black shadows under his eyes and he's acting like he's given up, Gran and Grandad are coming over too.

Gran takes one look at Dad and moves in that day for a few weeks, so at least we are eating proper meals again.

Dad was cross at first, he said that Gran shouldn't be looking after him and Mum at their age, if anything he should be looking after her, it should be her time to take it a bit easier. The order is all wrong, parents looking after their grown-up son when he can't cope, while his wife loses her mind, you can almost see more guilt settling heavily on Dad's shoulders like dust on a shelf, as Gran moves into our house.

However, the rest of us are past caring what Dad thinks, he needs the help, and we are relieved when he is signed off from work sick. He's sleeping a lot, and when Mum moves into Greenacres for a trial week we are all ready for a break from constantly watching her and trying to keep her safe.

Dad still insists on visiting her nearly every day, he is sad all the time but after almost disappearing into himself for a few days he is starting to talk. Gran is making him sit downstairs to eat and I can imagine him sitting at the table with Gran when he was a small boy, she knows how to speak to him to get the result she wants.

I have realised he will always be her child, and she will treat him in that way, it never occurred to me before that my parents are always seen as children by their parents.

The first night Mum comes back from Greenacres, Gran is still here. I can see Mum and Gran are both nervous, Mum doesn't know who Gran is, and Gran doesn't know what to do or say. They stalk around each other, and Mum is anxiously suspicious of this older lady, Dad has no idea how to handle it.

So, we solve this in the way we often solve things in our house, we all sit down in front of the television and talk about what we are watching on TV, to distract us from having to discuss anything awkward or uncomfortable.

We love quiz shows and are quite a competitive bunch, Catchphrase has us arguing with the TV in no time. It's a programme where an animated character pops up and acts out various phrases and sayings and you have to guess what they are. It's too difficult for Mum and she is getting frustrated because she can't understand what's happening, as we all become more animated shouting at the TV. When the music plays though, you can tell she recognises it as she hums tunefully along.

We leave Mum and Dad on their own and they watch Doc Martin, I don't think Mum knows what is going on, but she is happy to sit there calmly with Dad, like they used to do on a Sunday night before our ordinary week began.

Dad is looking better, and when Gran decides it's time to move back to her own house, she says she will miss us, but not Grease on repeat, she now knows the words to every song and can recite the dialogue, she's not sure what use that will be in her old age.

Mum is comfortable in front of the television watching her favourite films and musicals over and over again, the ones from when she was growing up. Sometimes I sit with her and it's as if she is watching them for the first time. She points at the screen and even smiles at some of the jokes, completely absorbed by the world inside the box.

It gives us time to do other things and it's a useful babysitter, Dad says it's the same as when Dan and I were children and we watched Thomas the Tank Engine on repeat, it nearly drove everyone mad.

A few weeks later and Mum is hoovering again that's the third time today, she forgets she's done it already and has no idea what time it is, she hoovers day and night, the house has never been so clean.

Dad and I know she is getting seriously worse, and we only leave her alone for very short periods of time now. Dad's company are understanding, and some of his work can be done from home, and my A levels mean I am not at school that much so I can help.

It's early evening when we leave Mum asleep and go out for less than two hours to my school for the university talk to discuss what I might want to study and where I could go. I can tell Dad wants to be here for this, he doesn't want to let me down. I think I know what I want to do but haven't decided for sure.

We joke on the way home about possible careers for me, coming up with ridiculous ideas about what I could do. It's more like the old times than it has been for ages, and we stop to pick up fish and chips.

The minute we enter the house, the smell of gas is overpowering. The gas burners on the cooker are all on and not lit, and Mum is desperately trying to strike a match to light one of them. Dad grabs the matches and turns off the burners as she screams at him to leave her alone, I open all the windows and we push Mum outside.

She perks up as she looks towards the road and we struggle to keep hold of her, grabbing her arms as she kicks out at us both, trying to break free to run towards the traffic. The next-door neighbours come out to see what's going on and quickly retreat inside.

Instead of Dad and I looking desperate, uncomfortable, and ashamed, we look at each other and laugh, it's the sort of thing we would have laughed at in a comedy show when it happened to other people. It is not funny this is our life, and we know that as we bundle Mum back inside, but it's another brief moment of madness thanks to this disease.

We make sure we don't leave Mum alone after that, it's exhausting being the full-time carers of an adult with Alzheimer's, on call day and night. Dad does most of it trying to juggle work whilst caring for Mum.

I am starting to dread being left on my own with her in case she does something I can't deal with, and that thought triggers the guilt inside me, surely the least I can do is give Dad some time off and look after my mum.

In my last session with Cassie, I realised I can't talk about Mum and how I feel about everything on demand, at the specific time when it fits with my appointment with Cassie, or when Dad tries to make some time.

Everyone thinks I should be able to switch it on and off, so ideally, I need to be feeling bad to suit their timetable and talk about Mum when they ask me to. I can't, I'm not being awkward even though I can tell they think I am.

Cassie is trying to understand and said I need to write down my feelings if no one is around to talk to, or if I can't say it out loud, then I won't forget, and we can work through it at our next appointment. I don't know if I can do that or if it will help, but I will try.

Living like this in my head makes me sadder, and I randomly go from wondering if I should do some shopping, to if Mum might die soon, in the space of one split second. My thoughts are chaotic and making me anxious as they push forward jostling for space one after another, crashing into each other with force, like snooker balls when you break. They are loud and distracting it's a constant background noise nobody wants to hear, or the soundtrack nobody wants to play. I need to find an off-switch somewhere.

A few weeks later Dad and I call to see Mum at Greenacres early in the evening while she is on another one of her trial weeks. Mum is upbeat today and I update her about my possible university choices, she nods and smiles and I know she doesn't understand a word I am saying, but it feels good to talk to her anyway when she is so calm.

As I sign out in the visitor's book, I notice that Dad was here yesterday, but he didn't mention it to me, and walking across the car park I wonder why.

When we get nearer to the car, I ask him about the visit. He looks uncomfortable and says he popped in briefly to see Mum and pick up Cassie because she had a problem with her car, and then he says that they went for a quick drink before he took her home.

I am out of the car across the car park and back up the steps like lightning, why on earth would Dad take Cassie for a drink and not mention visiting Mum yesterday?

As I storm down the corridor, I am furious at the injustice of it all, Cassie and Dad carrying on as if nothing is happening. Mum's life has disappeared before our eyes, and they have been out for a drink. I fling open Cassie's door and it bangs against the wall, she looks up, I have startled her, good.

"I want to know if the only reason you've been helping me is so you can see my dad I thought you were my friend someone I could talk to and trust without you going behind my back and passing everything I say on to Dad did you fancy Dad when we first came here the day you met him again or does it go further back than that to school I bet you were pleased when Mum came here so you could make a move on Dad I bet something happened before she came here and are you even allowed to see a residents husband you do know they are still married"

She tries to speak a few times, I am not interested, there is no defence, she has betrayed me and Mum, I storm out again back down the corridor, racing down the steps and out through the main gate, leaving Dad shaking his head and shouting after me in the car park.

It's like everything inside is at boiling point waiting to spill out, ready to explode at anyone about anything. Nothing makes me happy, and I know people try but what's the point of everything when she's not going to be here?

Maisy is kind but she doesn't get it either, our family of four has disappeared, a bomb has been dropped and exploded in the middle of our living room and we've all run to different corners to hide. Unable to connect to each other anymore, we can't even speak to each other. We retreat to our rooms as much as we can, badly wounded and barely focused on our own survival.

I head to the corner shop and buy a litre of vodka and a bottle of lemonade using Dan's old ID, then hop on the bus towards town keeping my head down.

I am on a mission to self-destruct, and I get off the bus knowing exactly where I am going as I cross the road to the park.

I sit in the middle of a crowd of bushes which we used to hide in and use as our den years ago. I want to obliterate all my thoughts and feelings, and I alternate between drinking and drunkenly sleeping, waking up regularly and wondering where I am as it gets darker and colder.

When I wake up for the last time it's 6am and I have drunk over half the vodka. I bin the rest and head for the public toilets to wash my face and pee, as I look in the mirror I recite idiot, idiot, idiot to my mirror image.

My phone is full of concerned messages, and a reminder for the university open day today pops up filling my screen with the future. I switch it off knowing that if I head to the station, I have time to get a coffee and make the train to London in plenty of time to pick up the connections to York.

I feel shit after all the alcohol, and I'm still in yesterday's clothes creased and dirty, but I am not going home to face Dad after my fight with Cassie. I will go to the open day on my own, it will be fine, I have already visited another two universities so I know what to do.

Random disturbing thoughts pile into my head as I wait at the station, what if I jumped in front of a train?

It could all be over if I took a big step at the right time.

It would be quick, then I wouldn't have to deal with anything ever again.

But what would happen to the driver, would he never drive a train again?

Would I ruin his life and his family's life?

Maisy's voice of reason comes into my head along with one of the quotes from a poster on her wall "The best is yet to come."

What if that is true and I'm going to miss the best part of my life?

The train pulls in and I get on, it stops me thinking, and I sleep for the first part of the journey. When I eventually get to York, I feel a bit better, at least I made it here.

I walk around the university and eat two muffins one chocolate and one blueberry, well it counts as fruit and the sugar helps, as I work out which sessions I want to attend.

I realise as I look around, I am not like these people with their parents in tow, excited and optimistic about being here. I am balancing on a tightrope with the possibility of falling off at any moment, constantly looking down into an unknown land below me.

I turn to walk back to the train station, stamping my feet on the wet pavement splashing my dirty jeans and making my way home again. I phone Dad before I board the train, he has been frantically worrying about me and I can hear the tension in his voice, he doesn't care about the fight and will be waiting on the platform at the station in Oxford to take me home.

He doesn't know what to say when he picks me up, he tries to get me to understand that he can't lose me as well, and drills into me that I must always pick up my phone.

I feel bad, but Cassie still sits heavily between us as another thing we can't talk about, and that's not my fault.

I message Maisy to rant about Dad and Cassie, but she is far too cross that I went off without telling her to listen to my side of things, this is possibly my lowest day and I mentally beat myself up about all the bad decisions I have made in the last 24 hours.

Two weeks before my 18th birthday, Dad's phone rings and he goes into the garden to take the call.

He comes back into the house looking nervous and announces there is a permanent place available for Mum at Greenacres, but she will have to move in the day before my birthday. They can't hold the place for more than two weeks as they have a long waiting list.

I wonder if desperate families out there are hoping someone will die soon, so a place will become available for their loved one, does somebody always have to die?

For the next two weeks, I flit between wanting time to go quickly and slow down at the same time.

When the night before Mum moves forever finally arrives, it is a bizarre night. Mum and I are dancing around the kitchen like we used to before she was ill, as The Bangles blast out their best tunes in the background. She is having some lucid moments as if she knows we need her to leave us with something positive to remember, so she gifts us this one final happy memory.

Mum is here with me, and for a few short minutes, she is my mum again.

For the rest of my life, I will love "Walk Like an Egyptian" because it will remind me of these precious moments.

I leave Mum still dancing in the kitchen and my tears start before I reach the bottom of the stairs, falling quietly in time with my upward steps, my mind and body are too exhausted to care who sees me cry now. Dad is at the top waiting to come down and starts to speak, we act out a polite manoeuvre at the top of the stairs to avoid touching each other, the way strangers would at their first dance class together, only as close as necessary, not wanting to make the wrong move.

I rush past him into my room, the unspoken no-go zone where nobody comes in uninvited anymore.

Mum would never have let us get away with this macho bravado, closing ourselves off and being reclusive in our rooms, all pretending we were fine. She would have made us talk about how we feel, but she's not here to sort us out and we don't know how to do it without her.

2018 - Mike

As I pack Maggie's bags for the last time, Maggie's private places aren't so private anymore. Precious things including a heart-shaped pebble that only means something to her, and birthday and Christmas cards from the boys throughout the years all go in.

Going through her underwear drawer is too personal, trying to choose what she should take while wondering if she will care. I conclude she always cared before Alzheimer's so I should care on her behalf. I neatly fold everything, even if no one else notices, it feels like the right thing to do for Maggie.

I try to imagine her new space with some of our possessions in it and start to urgently run from room to room gathering memories in picture and ornament form from our life together, proving our shared history. Each one is a reminder of a person or place, and looking at the empty space they leave, pushes my thoughts deeper towards the raw pain of what I am losing.

In a strange way, it helps to feel useful, I can't pack everything, and I use the practical skills that come easily to me to complete the task as my brain kicks back in. I have a deadline to meet and a job to do and I need to focus solely on getting the right things into that room for her. When I have finished, four large suitcases wait expectantly by the door ready for tomorrow's journey.

I had been trying to keep from the boys how difficult I was finding moving Maggie into Greenacres, casually talking about it as the next step in the process and insisting it would be easier to take her on my own.

And it turned out that the build-up was a lot worse than the event itself and when I took her in and returned alone it was surprisingly uneventful. Maggie was in familiar surroundings after all the previous visits, and she settled quickly on that first day. I left the staff fussing over her, admiring her photographs, and slipped away to cry with relief in the car park.

I sat there for some time until I felt able to drive home.

It doesn't feel like this is forever, it just feels like any other visit.

2018 - Sam

Dad and Maisy have been planning my birthday without my knowledge. When I get up on the morning of my 18th Maisy has arrived, and they are sitting at the kitchen table together looking pleased with themselves. I can see they are willing me to be alright today, after Dad took Mum in yesterday, I know it matters to them that I have a good day. Dad wanted to go alone, and I didn't argue.

I hadn't given my birthday much thought, we had enough going on getting everything ready to move Mum.

They have arranged for us all to go out for breakfast, and I eat the biggest stack of pancakes covered in strawberries, maple syrup and cream as Dad hands me a silver envelope.

He has booked a hotel in London for me and Maisy for three nights as his present, and we have tickets to see Drake courtesy of Maisy. I can't believe they have sorted this out for me and I genuinely smile at how special this makes me feel.

Maisy and I get the train to London that afternoon and enjoy getting lost in commuter land, fighting our way through the station as people head home for the weekend, we are fish swimming the wrong way up the river.

We head for the hotel, check out our room which has an awesome view across from the London Eye, drop our bags and go out to eat. It's all very grown up, Maisy giggles frequently, we have never stayed away together in a hotel, and I try not to feel awkward as we hunt for a restaurant in a city that is not familiar to either of us.

We spend time by the river drinking coffee, eating croissants, and trying to avoid the persistent pigeons. We cross the roads with caution as if we have just learnt this skill, trying not to get mown down by electric taxis we can't hear, great for the environment but not so good for the dead body count.

When we go into the Tate Modern, I can imagine Mum here loving the modern art, wanting to challenge herself to find something interesting in everything she looks at while I struggle to understand it. I guess the art you enjoy changes like the books you choose to read when you get older.

It is an amazing weekend, a world away from where we live although it's not far on the train, we haven't visited London much growing up. We immerse ourselves in every experience and become excited tourists going to every free thing on offer, and there is a big choice.

The relief I feel from visiting somewhere with an unfamiliar labyrinth of streets is refreshing. There are no memories around every corner, it's all a blank page, but I do wonder how anyone ever found their way around here before Google Maps.

Seeing Drake was a highlight and as we jumped about and shouted our heads off, the adrenaline kicked in and I was totally present in the moment, for the first time in ages nothing else was edging its way in.

Neither of us wants to go home, we have had the best time and it has given us some space to be us, Sam and Maisy, the ordinary young couple, without the weight of the labels that we carry with us as part of our real lives.

Maisy's handbag is stuffed full of every free thing she could find, the hotel toiletries are her favourite along with the hotel biscuits. It makes me laugh on the train home when the zip breaks on her bag and it seems the freebies are going to cost her after all.

Dan is home for the weekend, and exactly a week after my birthday a letter arrives addressed to Dad.

He opens it in the kitchen as soon as he gets in from work and urgently shouts us down from our rooms. We jostle each other with elbows out on the stairs, we are six and eight again, competing to get there first.

We arrive breathless to find Dad frozen to the spot in the middle of the kitchen, hands shaking, with tears streaming down his face.

He moves to the table and motions for us to sit down, then he gives the letter to Dan, it's from Mum.

None of us can make eye contact or read it out loud, and as it passes around our little circle of three our tears fall silently into puddles on the kitchen table.

Mum

So, I have moved into the nursing home, I hope I wasn't too terrible to you all before you decided the time was right for me to go. I wanted to write this while I still could, it's 2015 as I write, and I wonder how many years I managed to stay with you at home.

Mike, Daniel, and Samuel, you can tell what I am saying must be important, it's either important or you are in trouble boys when I use your full names! You are what I live for, you are more than I could ever have hoped for in my life. Boys, from meeting your dad my life changed forever. I didn't realise it was possible to be so happy, to feel completely understood and valuable to someone else. Mike, you know how strong our love is, you showed me how to love and be loved, you are the other half of me.

Boys, I will always be your mum, your biggest cheerleader, even when I might not recognise you or be here at all, know I am watching over you. I will never leave you as I am inside your hearts, and my heart bursts with pride every time I call you my sons. I know you will be sad and mourn for what we had, our life before I was ill. It often felt to me like we had the perfect family life, the one from TV with a happy Mum and Dad and two perfect children.

When it is hard, remember all those times we laughed and couldn't stop, and all the special holidays we had when you were little. Sam, you always made us laugh with your impressions, especially in public waving your jazz hands and doing funny walks, we attracted attention everywhere we went. Dan your obsession with trains was legendary. I remember the train fancy dress we made from painted cardboard boxes that you insisted on wearing at the holiday camp three years running. And how it was so wide Dad had to lift you through every doorway! These are our unique stories to pass on and talk about, our family tales to remember forever to keep the memories alive.

A bit of advice while I can think clearly enough to offer it. Find someone that not only lets you be yourself but encourages you to be the best version of you, who lets you be vulnerable and who gently pushes you to want to do more to be a better person. Do things now, don't wait for a different day, more time, or better weather because putting it off means it might never happen, and if it matters to you make it happen, we all know how short life can be.

Now, this is important. I know you will be finding it difficult to talk to each other about your feelings, but you must. You are the best support for each other, and I insist you all make an effort, do not hide from what has happened or bury it somewhere deep inside or it will come back and bite you later on. You need to deal with it in your own way but not on your own. And you need to carry on finding your own lives again, ones you want to live, otherwise, all the work Dad and I put into bringing you up is wasted. Let people help you to work through whatever you need to, and be there for each other, love each other fiercely, that would be the best gift you could give to me now.

Finally, boys don't let Dad stay on his own forever, he needs to move on with his life too. Looking after me will have been devastating for him as he gradually watched me disappear. Apart from that, I know he will be hopeless on his own!

Always know my life has been amazing because of you. I love you all more than you could ever know, my family.

Mum xx

It shouldn't be a surprise to any of us that Mum is still here in charge, sorting us all out, and the last thing she can give us is the letter to make us talk, to help us to grieve together and accept what has happened. And it works, we try to open up and we joke about Mum, talking about the past with some humour for the first time in a long time as we share a few drinks.

I thought it was just me who had things I wish I'd asked Mum before it was too late. Lots of questions that can never be answered about her life in the past and how she saw my life developing in the future.

Things I wish I had said to her more, like telling her how much I loved her, it turns out we all feel this way.

We talk about those things and support each other, tell each other it's okay and privately know however much time we'd have had with Mum, as Mum, it would never have been enough.

By about nine o'clock we are all cried out and choose to go our separate ways for the rest of the night. Dan heads up to bed, he has an early train back to uni in the morning, and I leave Dad sitting in the kitchen and head to Maisy's feeling lighter than I have in months.

Tomorrow is my first visit to Greenacres since Mum moved in, I've been putting it off. Dan's not been either, we didn't discuss it before he went back to uni but I know he feels the same, he doesn't want to go.

They said to give her a chance to settle in and us a chance to begin to adjust, I was relieved, it gave me permission not to visit. Fear is sweating out of me when I arrive, I'm sure they must be able to smell it as I hop from foot to foot trying to shake off the adrenalin while walking past the people in the reception area.

Dad is perfectly calm and grabs my hand to slow me down. I keep taking deep breaths and puffing out my cheeks to keep the oxygen going around. If you didn't know where you were you could easily mistake this place for a hotel with polished floors, high ceilings, a big glass chandelier and smiley faces behind the reception desk, sparkly clean and ready to impress.

It's different dropping Mum off for a visit knowing she will come home again; this visit marks the start of spending the rest of our lives apart. I am a teenager visiting my mum who is living with people who are all strangers, most of them have the same problem as her, they are just older, unpredictable, and frightening. I don't want to say or do the wrong thing.

Nothing prepares me for what I find when I open the door to the communal lounge, they are all singing and it's not great musically speaking. They are all facing me lined up like a choir, and my mum is at the front, clearly somewhere else in her mind, as she looks straight through me, she looks happy, they all do. Maybe they only wheel in the happy ones for this.

We had to give them some photos before Mum moved in to hang on the door to her room, to show the outside world how she existed before Alzheimer's took over.

One photo was quite recent from her last day of teaching, she was in a red dress it was one of her favourites. Two of the photos have us all on, one from a family holiday and one taken with our garden in full bloom in the background. The final one was of Mum and Dad alone on their last holiday on top of a mountain somewhere when she knew she was ill, but she still looked like my normal mum.

As I walk towards Mum's room, I don't see old people when I stop outside each closed door to look at their photos.

Their photos belong to different versions of the people I've just seen singing. I see their stories, and photos of their lives before this disease when they were younger, a dentist, a scientist, and a postman live here, all these other lives.

Next to their job photos are family pictures similar to ours, full lives edited into four photos and a short paragraph about them and their previous life. These were vital important people, it's so cruel they end up here. It brings them to life for me though, and it gives me a glimpse of who they were, making them seem more normal.

Mum is normal in here, not the odd one out anymore in a sea of normal people at home and in the outside world, she is in the right place. This disease doesn't discriminate it doesn't care whose life it destroys it could happen to anyone.

I go into Mum's room with its big window and a good view of the garden, and it's a florist's shop. It's full of all types and colours of flowers, and the smell is overpowering, everyone has sent flowers to welcome her here, or maybe to ease their conscience so they don't have to visit.

I go and sit in the brown leather club chair in the corner that used to be in Mum and Dad's bedroom and wonder how many days of my life I am going to spend here. Her room is a mini version of our house, with pictures from home on the walls, even the rug from the lounge has made its way here. It suits Mum, it's cosy and comfortable, and it's nothing like the clinical hospital room I sat in when I broke my ankle, it's feeling more like her home now.

When I get home, I go into our garden for the first time in over a week and spot something underneath the overhanging willow tree in the far corner. Our garden has always been a random experiment with colourful plants dotted everywhere in the spring and summer without any plan. It's like they've all been thrown up in the air and grown happily where they landed.

Mum enjoyed the garden, and it has carried on respectfully in her absence, doing its own thing, transforming itself as the seasons changed. A moving painting viewed through the frame of our kitchen window.

As I get closer to the tree, I realise it's Mum's penguin slippers sitting there soaking wet, they are so small, she has tiny feet, they obviously didn't make it to the nursing home.

I think about Dad a few weeks ago writing Mum's name inside all of her clothes like she used to do in my school uniform. It makes me wonder if we all eventually return to the helpless children we once were through illness or old age and need someone to care for us again.

Almost everything else belonging to Mum has gone with her, or we packed it into boxes and took it to the charity shop acknowledging that this time only one of us was moving house. Mum was very clear with Dad a few years ago, she didn't want him to return home and try to live surrounded by her ghost from the past.

As I stand in the garden and look around, my 16th birthday comes rushing back, that's where it all started for me. It seems like a lifetime ago and we've all had to move on to places I could never have imagined inhabiting before.

2018 - Mike

I think there must be something wrong with me. I am bouncing up the steps into Greenacres to visit Maggie when I realise the spring in my step is not only because I am happy that Maggie is settling in well, it's also because I am hoping I will see Cassie again here today.

This is starting to feel like it could be more than a friendship feeling. We've been for a few coffees, and I am thankful she has helped Sam to work through his feelings but how can I possibly be thinking this way?

Is it wrong to think like this, probably yes, I feel confused and guilty and head down a rabbit hole of possible scenarios, none of which end well.

Should I mention something to the children?

I am still married, does this mean I need to be alone until Maggie dies?

Am I simply lonely and Cassie has been there for me?

I conclude that I can't discuss how I feel with Sam and Dan, it would be wrong and there is nothing to tell them, and I don't know how Cassie feels, how stupid am I?

I've been talking to Cassie because I feel so alone and she understands, she is easy to talk to. Now I can't talk to her because it's about her, I can't talk to anyone.

My mood drops as each potential solution ends at a cul de sac and my brain bounces about uselessly making me more frustrated and cross with myself. No one will ever replace Maggie. She talked about this happening when she was first diagnosed and I protested it would never happen, but she knew I would need someone, she even mentioned it to the boys in the letter. It is too soon, although I don't know when it would be acceptable to try and build a new life for myself.

Logically, I lost my Maggie years ago, bit by bit, until nothing recognisable was left. I think unconsciously I had started letting her go over the last few years to survive the inevitability of living with the ever-emerging stranger, being her carer felt similar I imagine, to being a widower but without the body.

2018 - Maisy

I went to Greenacres with Sam today and after saying "Hi" to his mum I left him alone with her. I think she wants to talk to just him sometimes, Sam says she doesn't mind if we are both there but I'm not so sure.

I ventured into the main lounge and met Mrs Brown on the way in, and she ushered me loudly to a specific chair. In any other environment, this would be normal, like being shown to your seat at the theatre, but Mrs Brown was a headteacher and she thinks she is still directing her pupils much to the annoyance of some of the other residents. I get the feeling she is not popular when lots of eye-rolling is happening behind her back.

I am seated at a large round dining table and Mrs Brown sits down next to me, instructing me on today's task, which is to complete a large jigsaw. We are apparently building it as part of a school project, to learn more about famous painters. She has a comprehensive knowledge of Monet and asks me questions, answering them for me as well. I smile and nod and try to remember the last time I sat still and did a jigsaw; it was the Christmas before Dad left and I'm sure I was nearly ten.

There is an order and a plan to jigsaw building that I have lived without knowing until now. It's the corners first followed by the straight edges, they must be complete before we are allowed to move on and group the remaining pieces into colours, then we can start to fill in the middle. I am absorbed in my task, and we work side by side silently concentrating as the image of waterlilies begins to emerge. Mrs Brown is quicker than me and when I put a correct piece in she gives me a smiling nod of approval, I think I would have liked her as a teacher.

We must have been sitting there for over an hour when Sam appears with his mum, he is ready to go so I say my goodbyes.

I look at these people thrown together by what has happened to them, what must it be like living with people you don't know?

I wonder if they are familiar to each other, and do they think they are their family now or do they wonder where their family are, and why they left them here?

Mrs Brown jolts me from my thoughts as she shouts after me that we will finish the jigsaw in our next lesson. I am surprised to find myself looking forward to it, and I send her my best smile across the room, and she smiles back.

2018 - Sam

Today I went to visit Mum for the third time, it was the first visit to Greenacres on my own, without Maisy or Dad, and it took me a while to stop overthinking what I might find, and wondering how I would deal with it alone.

However, it was starting to feel like a wasted visit, because Mum had had a bad night and they didn't want me to go in and disturb her, she needed to sleep. I was so far out of my comfort zone standing in reception and turned to leave, trying not to look at or speak to anyone, when a man at least thirty years older than Mum appeared by my side and said, "Aye up lad, you look like a rabbit caught in the headlights, come and sit over here, I'm Bert by the way."

I turned and looked at him and he was the sort of grandad you see in a children's storybook; he could easily play Father Christmas. He was dressed in smart black trousers, a white shirt with a bowtie, and a striped blazer with shiny black shoes completing the look, he was dressed for going out.

Bert starts to tell me some of the highlights from his life story, it turns out he was a pianist in a band for years, and after his wife died, he went on to play solo in local hotels and bars just to get him out of the house. We talk about music and Bert talks about some bands and artists I have heard of including Elton John, one of Mum's favourites and Jerry Lee Lewis, it's weird to think we know some of the same stuff.

I follow him to his room, and he shows me his record player, it's in pristine condition. He says he is only allowed to use it at certain times as it needs to be quite loud because he can't hear that well, but neither can most of the other residents, so he doesn't know why it's a problem.

His room has framed pictures up everywhere some of him at the piano, one with his wife on a ship and lots of garden pictures including big vegetables and a black and white terrier-type dog. Snapshots of younger Bert in his happy life, before he ended up in here living this one.

I show him my phone and explain about music streaming, he can't work out how so much music can be on one small phone, and he keeps turning it over in his hands. He makes me demonstrate how it works and apprehensively I put my headphones close to his whiskery ear, his smile is worth every bit of my discomfort, and he makes me laugh when he says "I can't believe it" repeatedly in his booming voice while pulling a shocked comedy face.

When I leave Greenacres I realise I am whistling, and the tension I felt when I arrived has gone from my body, I stretch and flex my back, pushing my shoulders down as I breathe slowly and calmly feeling I have achieved something by visiting on my own.

As I walk back down the steps, I wonder why Bert is in here, but I know I won't ask him, I don't want to know.

A few days later Maisy and I are in a charity shop in town. She doesn't mind where her clothes come from, if she wants something and she can afford it she will buy it. She often trawls from one local charity shop to another, looking for quirky alternative stuff she can sew things on to or chop to pieces. From when it leaves the shop to when she wears it it's transformed in some way, t-shirts are her speciality, you would never recognise them. I love how confident she is to be Maisy, to stand out and not change or hide anything about herself to fit in with anyone else.

Anyway, instead of following her around feeling awkward as usual, I wander over to some old records and start to flick through them. I am nearly at the end of the stack when I see Piano Hits of the '50s and '60s and I nearly jump with excitement. I know exactly who will love this one and take it over to the till to pay.

2018 - Mike

"It's only a friendship at the moment, however, I think it might be more than that in the future and I want you to know because I don't want you to feel left out like you did when Mum was diagnosed, and we didn't tell you. I am probably doing the wrong thing, but I don't know what the right thing to do or say is. I've spoken to your gran, and she thinks I should tell you even though there is nothing to tell you yet."

This comes out as one quick sentence, not at all the way it did when I rehearsed it privately to the mirror. I watch as Sam gets up to leave the kitchen, after banging his fist on the table and pushing his chair back knocking it over, while his face gets redder.

The boys never swear in front of us and when Sam uses the f-word it is more of a shock than the shouting and the violent door slamming. I know they all swear with their friends, but they never have at home, and we liked it that way it felt respectful somehow. I feel as if I have been punched in the stomach, I have done the wrong thing again.

An hour later Sam reappears in the kitchen, he says he is sorry, and he knows how hard it has been for me and he genuinely doesn't want me to be lonely. He carries on to say he is worried about leaving me when he goes to uni and asks me not to rush into anything, and I sit there and say nothing and wonder who the parent is now.

Cassie and I meet for a drink at a pub well away from home and Greenacres, much further out of town. It's not that I don't want to be seen with her, but I don't want the awkward questions if either of us meets anyone we know.

The first thing she asks me is if I got the letter from Maggie, apparently Maggie had given it to her when she first chose the nursing home and had made her promise to post it the week after she moved in permanently. Cassie doesn't know what it says but she is relieved it has arrived as Maggie was adamant about its importance. I don't want to share the details of the letter with Cassie yet, maybe I will in the future, but it is still too raw.

We chat about nothing of significance, and it is great to have a conversation not fraught with emotion or involving a decision. We are friends and nothing has happened between us, but we have acknowledged that we enjoy each other's company and want to spend more time together. As we leave, we arrange to meet again next week, and I am starting to be able to look forward a week at a time without dragging all the sadness along with me.

Sam and I are communicating better, and I don't want to jeopardise that. It surprises me that we have found a new normal so quickly. Maggie has barely been at Greenacres for two months and our routine has already formed a regular pattern as we adapt to the changes.

I think being back in the office is helpful for me, now the initial awkwardness of everyone being sorry and not knowing what to say has passed. Having colleagues around again with some office banter and structure to my week is what I needed. It's not long until Sam leaves and things will alter again, he has changed in the last few years, and grown into a new version of himself.

I want him to go to university so his new adventure can begin, and he can leave home like any other 18-year-old, with him being the main focus in his life again.

He has been through so much, both boys have, I am proud of them, and I'm remembering to say these things out loud as I am slowly learning how to be both Mum and Dad now.

2018 - Sam

We are sitting on the wall outside our school waiting for the doors to open into our new lives. Well actually, we are waiting for the gym doors to open so we can collect our A-level results, and I realise this is probably the last time we will all sit here together.

We must have waited for each other hundreds of times on this wall over the last seven years, it's feeling like an iconic place to me. It is one of those places I will remember clearly in the future in my panic dreams, when fear takes over my nightmares, playing out the same scene again and again and I wake up sweating and confused, unable to remember where I am. The dream will reoccur when I'm taking my exams and at other times of stress when I am stuck on this wall, glued to it, unable to move. My legs won't function, and I know I am late for an exam or an appointment, I can't move, I am paralysed to the spot in my reoccurring nightmare.

Today as I look up, the doors hit the wall and bang open and we all pile in.

Shaun opens his results first carefully opening his envelope, and of course, he's got what he needs to get into Oxford he doesn't look surprised. I've got what I need too, by some miracle I've got the grades. I don't feel the relief I expected to, it's a good feeling, but nowhere near the most important thing I think about in my life. Maisy opens hers and the relief is obvious to see after the ordeal of her mocks, we all breathe out as she breathes out and are hugging and jumping around with her as she tries unsuccessfully to hide her tears.

We phone home on speakerphone and celebrate with each other's parents. Maisy's mum cries, Shaun's mum "knew he would do it" and my dad says "I wish she could share this moment with you" at which point I nearly lose it. I am painfully aware of all the things she won't be there for, my graduation, my wedding, my children, and helping me choose my first house.

I will never share my life with her as an adult. I know we would have enjoyed spending time together and she would have helped me to open up, be vulnerable, and confide in her if things weren't going well. I also know Dad and Dan will be by my side and I will be there for them in our new style of relationship, as we tentatively step forward and start to share our feelings.

Everyone who comes into my life in the future will know how wonderful my mum was because I will tell them. I know physically she is still here and maybe I shouldn't think like this, but the battle inside me has ended and mentally I've accepted that she isn't coming back, and I don't think it's selfish anymore to want to move on with my life.

Maisy and I are becoming regular visitors at Greenacres, the staff say that everyone looks forward to our visits. I always go to see Mum first and then call in on Bert.

When I gave him the record, he ruffled my hair like I was twelve and it wasn't too awkward. He put it on immediately and started dancing ballroom style with his pretend partner and I watched the years drop away from him. He doesn't care what anyone thinks, I admire that about him.

Maisy joined Mrs Brown in the lounge as usual, that's why the other residents like her visiting, she is the only one who stops Mrs Brown from barking orders at them. We don't know her first name everyone calls her Mrs Brown and if we did it would feel disrespectful to use it somehow. They always find a jigsaw and it keeps them both quiet for hours, Maisy says she is learning new things about painting styles and different artists and enjoying it, Mrs Brown will never stop teaching.

2018 - Dan

I have been busy, it's not an excuse, it is an excuse, who am I kidding?

It's easier being away because I can pretend life at home is normal, old normal before Mum got ill. As soon as I come home the spell is broken, reality is right in front of me and avoiding it is not an option.

Dad has been great, I think he understands I needed some distance, some time to process everything and think about the last few years. I'm dreading visiting her, Sam's been going regularly he's stepped-up Dad says.

When Sam picks me up from the station with Dad, I do a double take, I almost don't recognise him. He's changed his hair the tramlines have gone, and he's grown taller in the last few months while I've been hiding away at uni. His hunched almost apologetic stance has gone too. He looks me straight in the eye and waves and I can see his life has started to move on. He is no longer stuck in the place he was when I left him.

Dad and I spent over a year hiding Mum's condition from him, trying to protect him and keep his life the same for as long as possible, I still don't know if we did the right thing.

He's chatting about his A levels and Maisy and updating me about Mum and the nursing home. I am entering back into the world I happily left behind and it is unrecognisable from when I left it, I feel like an outsider now. He has an easy confidence when he speaks and an optimism I haven't seen in him before.

We call at the pub on the way back from the station for one drink, and Dad tells us for the hundredth time that this is where he came with Mum on their third date, at least some things don't change. Then we head over to the nursing home, and I feel apprehensive and a bit sick as I face up to visiting Mum in her new home for the first time.

2018 - Sam

Dan looks like I did when I first visited Mum, scared to death. For the first time in my life, I feel like the older brother, as he looks to me for what to say and do, he doesn't know how to act with these people, and I do.

I can see how shocked he is when we go in and find Mrs Brown on good form shouting again. Cassie finds us almost as soon as we arrive, and we follow her down the corridor to find Mum. Dan is lucky Mum is not too bad today, she is smiling and excited about something. From her appearance you wouldn't know anything is wrong, her hair and makeup have been done for our visit, so she looks like an over glamorous version of our mum.

Mum has a secret, and it takes me ages to understand with Cassie's help, that she is trying to tell everyone, that she knows Mrs Brown's first name although I am not sure she understands what she is saying.

We play along with Mum, she is delighted with herself, and we learn that her name is Arabella, it is the only word Mum says for the first half hour of our visit, Maisy will be pleased to find out. At times like this, it is easy to imagine Mum at school herself as she twinkles and fizzes with mischief.

We take her for a walk around the garden and Dan relaxes as soon as we get outside, he starts to update her about his life. I hear it for the first time too and it is a world away from the life I have been living here. I'm not sure Mum is listening, it doesn't matter though she won't understand, but Dan needs to do this to try to connect with her again.

I wonder if I will change as much as Dan has when I go to uni, he sounds like a proper grown-up full of new ideas and opinions I don't recognise, I have never heard him talk so much about anything.

I meet Shaun in the evening and watch amused as he takes the gherkin out of his burger in silent protest as I forgot to ask for his meal without it. We have what I look back on as a very grown-up chat.

It's the first time we talk openly about our lives over the last few years and how everything made us feel, and it's the first time we listen to each other without the jokes and try to understand what the other one must have gone through. Maybe the conversation happened because we are going away to different places soon, and there was important stuff between us we'd both been ignoring.

Perhaps it was because we felt time was running out and we wanted to draw a line under our old lives ready for a new start.

Either way, it was refreshing, and we promise each other we will talk and visit regularly when we are at uni.

We walk out of McDonald's more adult than when we went in, and I try to imagine what my new world will be like without Shaun in it nearly every day, and I digest the new us, and think about all the changes to come.

Over the last two years I've grown up, I've not had a choice. I'm not proud of how I was when it all started straight after the party, how I reacted and how selfishly I behaved, I was another person back then.

Mum and Dad were not only my parents they were a double act finishing each other's sentences and they would have been together for life. Accepting Mum's diagnosis as a son was devastating and I am starting to understand what the loss of Mum means to Dad.

Life is not a perfect puzzle, it's messy and complicated, and all the pieces don't fit together easily as I wanted them to. There is no absolute end to our situation, life goes on and we all have the same 24 hours in our day, I've learnt to value mine more than I did before.

I will be at uni in September, the same one as Maisy, we've survived the worst time of my life, and I'm not about to give her up now.

Dad is moving on as well, I still don't like it, I like her, Cassie, but it seems too fast. Maisy says it will always feel too soon and I should know by now that life is too short to hang around waiting, if you have a chance of happiness, you should grab it with both hands, it's a quote from another one of her posters.

Mum has settled in and that's good, it is her home. Alzheimer's progressed rapidly for her, from the initial diagnosis to where she is now, she is in a world of her own, and no one can reach her and connect her to her past anymore.

It's easier for Mum, she doesn't remember who we are, but it's harder for me.

Sometimes before I walk into Greenacres, I see her through the front window and for a moment I see my mum, not the stranger she has become. It's like my brain stalls and needs a few seconds to adjust itself and reset to what is now reality.

I don't think the pain of losing her will ever go away, I will carry it with me for the rest of my life, perhaps that's normal for everyone when they lose their parents. I see Dad's mixed emotions flicker across his face when Mum starts to sing. She still loves music and remembers the words to songs from when she was younger, especially bands from the time she was dating Dad. I'm not sure the older residents appreciate the singing though when Grease regularly features.

I visit every week and so does Dad, Dan goes when he's home, his life is elsewhere and mine will be soon. Dad says Mum would be so proud that I got my A levels and first choice of uni, but more than that she would be proud of the person I have become.

I am going to be a nurse and Maisy is too. Mum's disease has taught me a lot, and maybe I will work with people with Alzheimer's in the future, I hope so, making a difference in their lives and conquering the world, one patient at a time.

Maggie

I don't know who I was,
I don't know who I am,
who is Maggie?

Acknowledgements

Thank you to my husband Craig Measom for his continued support, encouragement, and plenty of editing.

Daniel Wake, Alisia Angel, Holly Feeney and Sophie Wake for sharing childhood experiences and bringing their past to life.

James Wake for being an early reader, your opinions are always insightful. Thank you to my other early readers Alice Millard, Fiona De Mowbray and Sharon McWilliams for kindly ploughing through the early version and Fiona McKenzie for proofreading.

Matthew Bird for his typesetting skills and endless patience. And to Michael Heppell and all at *Write That Book* where my writing journey started.

Most importantly thank you to four exceptional gentlemen - Geoffrey Lee, Ralph Wainwright, William Christie, and Michael Measom.